D0287634

THE INCLINE

Also by William Mayne

THE BLUE BOAT

THE CHANGELING

EARTHFASTS

A GAME OF DARK

THE GLASS BALL

A GRASS ROPE

THE HILL ROAD

THE HOUSE ON FAIRMOUNT

THE OLD ZION

PLOT NIGHT

RAVENSGILL

ROYAL HARRY

UNDERGROUND ALLEY

WILLIAM MAYNE'S BOOK OF GIANTS

WILLIAM MAYNE'S BOOK OF HEROES

THE INCLINE

William Mayne

5-CHEVY CHASE
JUV.
c. 1

FEB8 1973

E. P. DUTTON & CO., INC.   NEW YORK

First published in the U.S.A. 1972 by E. P. Dutton & Co.
Copyright © 1972 by William Mayne

All rights reserved. No part of this publication may be
reproduced or transmitted in any form or by any means,
electronic or mechanical, including photocopy, recording,
or any information storage and retrieval system now
known or to be invented, without permission in writing
from the publisher, except by a reviewer who wishes to
quote brief passages in connection with a review written
for inclusion in a magazine, newspaper, or broadcast.

SBN: 0-525-32550-6   LCC: 72-75506
Printed in the U.S.A.
First Edition

Put her away, this doll of seasons
      Elapsed and succeeded,
Named and forgotten, played and done,

Elapsed and succeeded.
      Let her story rest that
On her wax face was recorded.

Put her away, this doll of seasons,
      Empty now of reminiscence;
After such life and voice

No more to speak of things
      Named and forgotten, played and done.
Time no more to recall how

Once those cheeks received
      Wonders now turned mortal,
Named and forgotten, played and done—

Softly impressed is softly lost.
      Elapsed and succeeded,
      Named and forgotten, played and done:
Dumb is the wax, its voices gone.

I

"ME WEAR a collar?" said Mason Ross, sitting up in bed and fingering the hard thing his mother had put into his hands. "Give up, Mam, it's not Sunday, and I don't want a collar for work. Folk don't work with collars on."

Mrs Ross opened the bedroom window and then stood away from it without saying anything. She turned her back to it and put her hands by her ears. The clock downstairs began to chime, twelve notes and then a silence, and then the first of seven strokes for the time of morning. Neither Mason nor his mother said anything. They both waited for something else. It happened at the fourth stroke. The air shook and the window rattled. The ground shook and the wardrobe rattled. Mrs Ross closed the window again after the explosion. Through the glass of it, however, there came the hiss of one of the steam cranes, now being moved to where the explosion had blasted another piece of hill out. It would be clearing and shifting rock the rest of the day.

"Don't maul that collar like that," said Mrs Ross. "It's to last you today, tomorrow and Sunday. And you aren't going to work, Mason, you're going into business, and that's not the same thing. In business you wear a collar, not a neckerchief."

Mason put the collar down. "Not there," said his mother,

taking it up again. "You'll sit on it." She put it on the chest by his bed.

"I'm not in business yet," he said. "They mightn't take me."

"You'll still want the collar for Sunday," said Mrs Ross.

Mason got up. It was the third, or fourth, least ordinary day of his life. It was the fourth if he counted the day he was born, but he could not remember that. It was the third if he began with the first day he went to school. He could remember thinking that day that he would never get out from the place, and he had been surprised when Mam had come for him and taken him home. The second, or next, most extraordinary day had been the day he left school, the last day of being there. Like the first day, it was one he had thought would never end; he had not expected to come out. Mam had not been there to take him home, of course, but the day had ended, and with it had ended his school life, suddenly, all over and done with. That had been yesterday. Today was probably going to be the start of his working life, the next thing that happened after school. He had not expected the collar. But there it was. He put it on, pushing the heads of the studs through the stiff lips of the holes and tying the black tie. When he got down the stairs and into the kitchen Mam pulled the tie and the collar off his neck and sent him to wash. While he was washing she damped the collar down again and ironed it hot and hard. Before he was allowed to put it on he had to clean his boots and put them on.

Then it was breakfast time. Mam put the teapot on the table, and stepped outside for a moment to call Dad, who was next door in the quarry office seeing about the worksheets and other papers.

8

"Still here, then?" said Dad, when he came in, with papers tucked under his left arm to be looked at while he ate.

Mason stood up at once and got ready to go, not wanting to be late, because if he was late today he could never catch up. It was not even going to be a proper working day; he was not sure that he would be taken on.

"Nay, sit down," said Dad. "You've plenty of time. You're in business, and that doesn't start while half past eight; it's work that begins at half past six, or six o'clock if you're on the gangs."

"I don't mind which I do," said Mason.

"Mebbe," said Mrs Ross. "But a quarryman's nowt if there isn't a quarry near by, but a business clerk can turn to any clerking trade, and be a known man."

"Well, there is a quarry," said Mason. Outside the house there was a whole quarry, the growing cliff backing into the hill, the long fingers of the tips with their bevelled ends, the flat cuttings where the rails ran, the building where the stone was sawn and faced and shaped, the mists of steam engines, the solid dark horses that themselves on cold mornings steamed like the engines, the trucks that they pulled, the tall chimney that like a random factory in the green broken fields where the quarry lay, smoked a gritty smoke. And, on the far side of the building and chimney, the automatic railway that ran down to the bottom of the valley and the sidings or dock.

"There's a quarry, right enough," said Dad. "But the stone gets further under every foot we drive back. There'll not be a quarry for ever, and if there's not a quarry there's nowt in the dale."

There was a knock at the door.

9

"Come in," Dad shouted. He was used to being interrupted at any time of day by messages out of the quarry. The visitor knocked again, but more nervously, and Dad shouted louder. The door opened, and a boy came in. It was Peter Ward, who had been at school yesterday with Mason, and who had started work in the quarry that morning. He wore a red neckerchief.

"Well, if it isn't a mucky quarryman," said Mam, cheerfully. Peter smiled.

"You daft devil," said Dad, "knocking on folks' doors; you can always walk in, Peter."

"That he can't," said Mam. "I have one quarryman walking in and I'll have them all, Bucko Robinson, Mad Jack, Annie Willy, and what-all else. No, you've to knock, Peter."

"Aye, he's a quarryman," said Dad. "I forgot."

"You just signed me up this morning, Mr Ross," said Peter.

"And have you earned your pay so far?" said Dad. "Are you worth keeping on?"

"I don't reckon," said Peter. "I've done nowt much but follow the gang and put some horse-muck in a barrow for the foreman. He just sent me with a message, but I don't know what it is, because I never heard most of the words before."

"You'll not even know where you're working," said Dad. "Sit and sup some tea, give him some, mother and I'll come on in a bit with you. Mason's off in a bit to see his work."

"I suppose he's going to work in a temple," said Peter. "It's not a Sunday and he's dressed in those clothes."

"He's going into business," said Mam. "The Vendale Savings Bank down in the village. He's to dress right for it."

Then it was time for Mason to stand up and be brushed hard with a clothes brush, to have his collar tapped firmly so that a sort of depression in it snapped out to a smooth curve, to have a quick rub at his left boot where a dull patch had appeared during breakfast, to have cold water put on his hair and another brush put through that. He was brushed everywhere.

Dad and Peter went out. "I'll be by after," said Peter.

"Wait of me if I haven't landed back," said Mason. Then he went out of the back door, the less dusty side of the house, and began to walk down the lane to the village.

The quarry was high on the hillside above the little town. The sun was up on the left, and it pierced among the houses with light and shade, so that each house and roof edge looked as if it might cut. Smoke rose from the houses and lay over them as if they were some metal object newly cast and laid in the valley, in the cloudy vapour of its own creation.

The slope of the hillside shut away the noise of the quarry. The noise of the town began to come to him instead, and the sound of the local insects, the sound of the shadowy dew splashing from disturbed grass on to his bright boots. He looked at his track behind him, darkening the grass.

The lane turned a corner and went straight down a rocky section. Here there was no sound from quarry or village. Only the bees and flies in the white roses and buttercups, elder and broom, trafficked noisily. The small coppery butterflies flashed in the sun; they lived here in clouds, like midges. Among the rocks that made the floor of the lane just here ran the channels of a beck; the water flashed up the blue glare of steel from ripple and rapid.

A wide field away to the right was the railway that mounted the hill from the dock in the town to the quarry. It was a slope laid on the irregularity of the hill, in some places dug into it, in some places banked above it. Down it would go a railway wagon full of stone, and up at the same time would come an empty truck. A wire cable joined the trucks, and ran up into the quarry buildings and over a great wheel and braked rims. The track was called the Incline. Now on it there was rising a wagon with one squeaking wheel. The descending wagon was out of sight in a cutting, but the empty one moved magically alone, with nothing apparently working on it, up the slope. Then it stopped for a moment while the brakeman at the top made some adjustments to the points away down at the bottom of the Incline, and the pulling wire quivered, and Mason saw it.

The truck sat there without moving. Someone shouted up from the bottom, and someone shouted from the top. The truck moved again and its wheel continued to squeal.

Beyond the Incline there was a wild, wooded, unused field. At the top of it the quarry tips reared up with great ends sloping a hundred feet to a skyline. Stone tipped there rumbled in long avalanches and slides, unsettled for days or months, unbound, dangerous. But seven hundred yards down the long wilderness there was a large new house, where Jedediah Spitalhouse lived, which he had built. Mason saw the private smoke of the house above the trees. He saw the gleam of its windows and the grey of its stone and the straight-run lines of its roofslates. The house was some sort of example for Mason of the difference between work and neckerchieves and business with hard collars with points that by now were trying to bite his Adam's apple out of his throat. Jedediah Spitalhouse had been at school with Dad, and they had both gone to work in the quarry on the same day. Jedediah had left quarrying and gone somehow into business and now owned most of the quarry and great numbers of other things besides. But Dad, staying in the quarry until his accident, would never have been more than a gang foreman if a chain had not broken and dropped seven tons of stone on his left wrist. He had lost his hand and his work, and had been able to do nothing for several years. But before Mason had been born Jedediah Spitalhouse had come to the town again and settled there, and found Dad and given him an over-seeing clerking job at the quarry, with a house.

That made Mason his own father's son, but a sort of descendant of Jedediah if he went into business rather than work.

Now he went on into the town to see what the business world was to be like. He came to the Vendale Savings Bank at twenty five minutes past eight, and stood outside it. The door was still barred and padlocked, and the windows blank. No one was about. Mason stood on the step and waited. He knew Mr Stewart by sight, but he did not know who else worked here. He had a feeling that Jedediah might appear and open the door, give him a desk to sit at and some money to do something with. The Bank might be the sort of business that Jedediah did.

A train came into the station and breathed out and out and out a long steam lung of breath. People came out of the station. The shop next to the Bank began to have its shutters taken down by a boy. He nodded to Mason and went into the yard behind the shop with the shutters.

A tall, yellow-featured man came up from the station and stopped at the Bank.

"Get off our step, lad," he said. "Go and laike in some other spot."

"I'm waiting of Mr Stewart," said Mason. "Half past eight."

"You'll wait on," said the man, not agreeably at all. "He'll be an hour yet, and then it's ten o'clock before the doors open. So be off with you."

"Yes Sir," said Mason, because there was nothing else he could do if Mr Stewart was not there. The man opened the door and went in, and closed it behind him. Once more Mason was waiting outside the shut door. There was a tapping on the glass window just along the wall. The yellow-faced man was knocking with his knuckles and waving him away. Mason got off the step and walked down to the station and the bridge.

There was nothing to do there. He could not cross the line because the level-crossing gates were shut. He turned away and walked along the track-side until he came to the dock at the bottom of the Incline. But he could not go close because of the dust. Some of it came from the stone sawn at the quarry and some from the trimming and working that went on here. He turned away from there and went up the hill and past the school.

Here the companions of yesterday were zoo'd behind the playground bars, looking out at him and shouting animal shouts. They still had a week and a half to spend at their desks. Those who left had their last day early and were always sent out top of the form. Then those that stayed behind had their own arrangements of who was top of the form, often quite a different matter.

The children who were left all looked very young, he thought. They shouted at him, "Parson Ross, Parson Ross," because of his Sunday-looking clothes.

"I'm in a Bank," he said.

"Aye," said some one of them, "School Bank," because that was the name of the hill he stood on.

The school bell rang and the noise of the yard drained

away into the school and an uncanny silence, as if all the children had vanished entirely, filled the yard and School Bank. The church clock, higher up the hill, said it was nine o'clock. The engine in the station made a wild reply with its whistle. In the school the piano played a fragment of unknown tune and the children began to sing a hymn that sounded unknown too. Mason had never heard prayers from outside before and it all sounded different, as if everything had been changed since yesterday.

He walked across to the high street and down towards the Bank again. He walked past it. The yellow-faced man was in there, working at some papers on a desk. Mason walked up and down the street five times, and on the fifth time he knocked at the door of the Bank and walked in. That was what happened at the quarry office. At the house the men knocked and waited. At the office they knocked and went in.

It was wrong here. The man stood up. "Now," he said, "that's plenty from you, coming in like that."

"It's Mr Stewart I've to see," said Mason.

"Mebbe and mebbe not," said the man. "But you don't walk in like that; you wait while you're asked. And you've not been asked."

"I have," said Mason. "Jedediah Spitalhouse told my Dad that I was to come at half past eight this morning to work here for Mr Stewart."

"He never did," said the man. "Not that."

"Yes," said Mason. "Just about, he said that."

"Aye, I'd forgotten you were to come," said the man. "But it's not to work; you mightn't be fit to work. You might be fit for nowt. Can you read and write?"

"Yes," said Mason. "I was top in class." He knew that did not mean much, but he knew he could read and write perfectly well, whole words at a time in either art, not like Peter Ward, who did not always remember all the letters and their sounds.

"It's an exam first," said the man. "You know what that is."

"A kind of big test," said Mason. "Aye."

"Sit at that desk," said the man, writing on a sheet of paper. "And this is the first question." He handed Mason the sheet of paper and a dry pen. "Copy that out and answer," he said. "Fill the whole page in quarter of an hour. When you've done it I have another for you." Then he turned back to his work. Dust from the box where the pen had been rose in the air and marked a ray of sunlight that bleached the desk. The man marked a page of a ledger, then turned out a cloth bag of copper coins, new and fresh, on to the desk, and counted them, two and two and two. The coins flickered like butterflies in the lane across the sunshine. The heap of coppers turned to nothing, leaving behind it a pool of silver money. In turn that flickered across the sunlight, like the beck water in the stones at the bottom of the lane.

Mason watched for a moment, which was all that the counting took, and then read his question.

"*What is an eccentric angle?*" it said.

Mason's mind found nothing to hold on to in the question. He had heard of some kinds of angle, like obtuse, or even Saxon, but eccentric angles were nothing he knew.

"I can't do it, please Sir," he said at last.

"Can't do it," said the man. "You must be able to do it; you're no sort of a clerk if you can't do that. What did they teach you at school? Everything but that, I suppose?"

"Mebbe," said Mason.

"You have to answer it," said the man. "But I don't want you to come off worst just because no one ever told you about something. When Mr Stewart comes he'll want to see your answers, so I'll write the answer to that one down for you, and you copy it out, then he won't know it's not all your own work."

"That's cheating," said Mason. "That's shinning, is that."

"You do what I say, and sharp too, before he comes," said the man. He took back his question and wrote below it, and handed it to Mason, who began to copy out what had newly been written.

Halfway through the task he began to feel uneasy about it. He had begun to write it one word at a time, thinking the second word a strange one, and the fourth odd, and the fifth impossible. He stopped and read the whole answer: "*To fish for salt herrings in soda water.*"

He remembered another sort of angle, besides Saxon and obtuse: to angle might mean to fish. "This is like a riddle," he said, while for safety, in case it wasn't, he finished copying it.

"Never in your life," said the man, reaching over and taking the answer he had written himself and putting it in his pocket. And then Mr Stewart walked into the office.

"Morning Lantho," he said. "Morning lad, who're you?"

"Mason Ross, Sir," said Mason, standing up.

"And what's he doing here," said Mr Stewart.

"Joking, Sir," said the man. "He is a droll fellow."

"Doing the examination," said Mason. "I think." He held up the paper he had written and Mr Stewart took it and read it."

"Very droll indeed," he said. "What does this mean, lad, and who are you?"

"Jedediah Spitalhouse sent him," said the man called Lantho. "By what he says."

"Jedediah told my Dad I'd to come at half past eight, and I came, and him, he's been giving me the examination, but I couldn't understand the question so he told me the answer and I don't understand that either."

"It's what Lantho thinks is a joke," said Mr Stewart. "But I think it's one joke too many, Lantho. This is your last day of business with me; when we close the Bank tonight you'll not be coming here any more. Mason Ross and I will manage by ourselves."

"If Mason Ross passes the examination," said Lantho. "Have you thought of that?"

"If he does," said Mr Stewart, "then off you go. If he doesn't, then I'll try another lad until I succeed."

Then he took Mason into another office and sat him at another desk. "We'll just see how you go," he said. "And we'll let Master Lantho sweat it out a bit. If he can use up some old joke like that on you and me, we can use up another old joke on him."

"Aren't you going to send him away?" said Mason.

"No," said Mr Stewart. "I'm just keeping him in order. Now, you listen, and answer these questions: they're real ones."

II

Mr Stewart handed Mason a paper. It was written out in Lantho's writing, and headed: "Examination of Mason Ross." Mason found that was puzzling, because Lantho must have known about the paper if he had written it out, and could have let him sit the examination as soon as he came, instead of first shouting at him to go away and then giving him a different question to make a fool of him.

"Go on, then, lad," said Mr Stewart. "Don't stare at it. Put down the answers."

"Yes Sir," said Mason. He picked up the pen on the desk and dipped it in the ink-well. The nib of the pen was new and the ink gathered in a black blister on its shoulders and would not come down to the tip. Mason shook the pen and the blister quivered and leapt off the metal and laid itself flat on the page and began to creep about the fibres of the paper.

Mason put brackets round it, after he had rubbed the back of the nib on the blot so that the ink spread better. The blot spread itself slowly out beyond the brackets. Mr Stewart read books of accounts and wrote with a silver pencil in them. Mason concentrated on the first question. It was simple addition and not difficult, because it was in ordinary numbers. Boys like Peter Ward found sums of that sort more difficult than sums about money or sheep or weights of stone, because to them there were not such things as numbers by themselves but only numbers of things. If the teacher said to them: "Add ten and twenty," they would say: "Ten and twenty what? please Miss."

The next sums became more difficult. Mason had to add together three or four numbers, subtract from them half another number and divide the answer by two thirds of the same number, and then say what that answer would be in ordinary numbers, if it were ounces, if it were pence, if it were inches, if it were seconds, if it were days starting on February the First 1901, and if it were square inches. Square inches are difficult, because a square foot, the next thing in size, has 144 in it, not twelve. Mason took a long time over that sum, and when he had done it he copied it all out again, complete with his workings in the margin, which is what he had been trained to do at school.

The next problem made him very unhappy. It gave a number, and asked him to do to it all the things he had just done to the previous answer, converting it from ounces, or pence, or inches, square inches, seconds and days. What really bothered him was that the number he was given was very near the number he had been working with before, and he wondered if there was a connexion. He wondered so much that he worked the previous question through again and came up with a different answer, but one still quite near.

He was about to work it a third time when Mr Stewart closed his books, put his silver pencil in his pocket, and called for Lantho.

There was no reply from the outer office. Mr Stewart called again, then got up and went through. When he came in again he left the door open. "Lantho has gone out," he said. "I don't know why. How are the sums going?"

"Middling," said Mason. He worked the sum a third time, and came up with his second answer and several left over. The fourth time he did it the answer came to the number given in the next question, and the fifth time it came again. He made a fair copy of that working, and then put the two exactly similar answers side by side.

There was a sum he could not do, about interest, and one about shares that he almost understood. Then there was a question that wanted him to give four reasons why cabbages are planted in straight lines.

He hardly dared to answer it, in case it was another of Lantho's tricks. He read it carefully a number of times, but it always read the same. Then he ventured to answer it. He thought that the ground would be easier to mark out with a straight string than with something curved; that it would be easier to remember where the seeds had been put; that it would be easier to hoe round things in straight lines. He could not think of a fourth reason.

Someone came into the front office. Mr Stewart went to see who it was. It was not Lantho, or a customer, but a note. Mr Stewart read it and laughed, and then stopped laughing and said "Oh dear," and looked solemn.

"Have you finished?" he asked Mason.

"I have, about," said Mason.

"You've used plenty of paper," said Mr Stewart. "Be off then and find Lantho. He's down by the bridge. Tell him it was just a joke about sending him off at the end of the day. He can be difficult at times, and tease other folk, but if you tease him back he doesn't take it well; he gets a bit petted. When you've found him and told him you needn't come back yourself."

"Haven't I done it right," said Mason. "All that figuring."

"I don't know how you've done," said Mr Stewart. "I haven't looked, have I? Look, I'll be having customers in here any time now, and I can't be looking at your work now. I'll write to you and let you know, and you'll maybe get the letter tomorrow if I want you to come on Monday."

Then he had no more time to talk. A customer came into the front office and Mr Stewart went to him as soon as he had picked up Mason's answers and put them in a drawer. Then he showed Mason out, holding the door open for him as if he were the bank's most important customer.

Mason came out into the bright street feeling that perhaps he had been an important customer that day. He half closed his eyes against the sunshine and the rising heat of the street and the dust and smell of a coal cart going past with its two horses, black sacks, and dirty man.

He was sure he saw Lantho at the top of the street, talking to someone else outside the cobbler's shop, but when he came close to the man, glad to be carrying messages and be dressed in the civil suit of business, he saw it was not Lantho, or anyone like him. His sense of being engaged on an errand went away from him at once, and he was just a warm person in a warm suit in a warm street, not really engaged in anything, not having any business that merited a business suit.

He was just turning away from the false object of his pursuit when he saw someone he knew and was glad to see. Jedediah Spitalhouse's daughter Moira was walking down the street with her governess. Mason thought of the governess as being called

22

Froyline, an unusual name. But Moira had told him it was the German word for Miss, and was spelt Fräulein.

Moira had always been a tiresome little girl, younger than himself, whom he had to play with at times when she sent for him. Then he had grown too old to be sent to play or be there when he was wanted, and he had not seen her for some time. Lately he had begun to wish he had known her better and not stopped speaking to her. He wanted now to know all about her and be interesting to her.

She came out of the Post Office, and he stopped to look at her and speak to her.

"Such curiosities, Fräulein," she was saying. Fräulein was about to say something in reply when Moira saw Mason and stopped being a person who talked about such curiosities and was a little girl again anxious to speak to people of her own age. She ran up the street towards him a little way, leaving a glove in Fräulein's hand. The hand, with the empty glove like another limp hand, stayed up in the air until Fräulein caught up with it.

"We're going to meet Mummy," said Moira. "At the station. Which way are you going? We're going down, of course, but I just wanted to come and talk to you. Stop it, Fräulein, I won't put it on until we get to the station, so don't pull. Walk behind, please."

Fräulein gave up the attempt to put Moira's glove back on, and walked behind. Moira did not walk but skipped.

"You do not comport yourself," said Fräulein.

"Let's run," said Moira, throwing her straw hat to Fräulein, taking Mason's hand, and running to the bottom of the street. After them came tall Fräulein cooing motherly, running as if she had feet but no legs.

"We came in the motor," said Moira. "Did you see it?"

"No," said Mason. "I was at work."

"Work?" said Moira. "But you're only about as old as me. You can't work."

"It's business, really," said Mason. "I don't have to do any more today, because it was just an examination to see whether I was good enough. I'll be in business in that bank there if I'm all right."

"Oh yes," said Moira. "I know about it. It belongs to Daddy, did you know? He owns some of it, some of the shares."

"Yes," said Mason, "people do share things. He shares the quarry too, doesn't he?"

"He shares and shares alike," said Moira. "My Mummy hates all that sort of thing, she's for the simple life. And I must say that I am too, quite often. I mean, I do love Fräulein in all sorts of ways, and I do love my lessons in Harrogate, and all the improving things, but simple things are so much simpler." Then Fräulein came up and began to mutter and reprove, until Moira kissed her and put on her hat and the loose glove.

"There's our new motor," said Moira, indicating with her whole hand, rather than pointing with one finger, the car in the station yard.

"*Der Zug,*" said Fräulein. "*Eilen sie.*"

"I beg your pardon?" said Moira. "You see, I won't let her speak German to me except in German lessons, will I, Fräulein?"

"You are very stiff," said Fräulein.

"Goodbye, Mason," said Moira, "you will have to come very soon and tell me all about Banks, because Daddy is sure to give me one some day."

"You can have mine," said Mason, generously. But by then she was being dragged away by Fräulein, unable to turn and wave and smile with any success.

Mason was now at the bottom of the street, where the station and the bridge were, where Lantho would be. He crossed the road that ran by the railway and then crossed the rails themselves and came on to the bridge. Lantho was not on the bridge at either side. Mason looked over and saw him by the mill leat, sitting in the grass on the bank. He called out: "Hello," but Lantho did not look away from the water. Behind Mason the train came into the station and started its own set of noises. Mason went down by the mill road and to Lantho, standing at the top of the slope and looking down at him.

"Hey," said Mason. "He says it's just a joke."

"Well, damn his eyes," said Lantho. "I know a joke. I know what a joke is, I can tell a joke when I see it. But when I can't tell whether it's a joke, then it isn't one. He can turn me off any time he wants, and he doesn't have to give a reason. So he's no right to joke about it. I don't call it a joke. You go back and tell him to damn his eyes."

"No, I couldn't," said Mason. "And his questions were about the same as yours, anyway."

"I know about the questions," said Lantho. "I've just come here to drown myself, because there's nothing much to life. And I still say damn his eyes, and your cheek for running his message. And I only work there by charity, the same as you will if you do."

"What do you mean?" said Mason. "It's business, not charity."

"I know it's charity," said Lantho. "That Spitalhouse put

25

me in the job, and he's putting you in too. But if he thinks that makes me his man he's wrong, and he should know it. He's taken more from me than he can give back, and he doesn't know how to treat what he got, either."

"It wasn't him that sent me," said Mason. He was startled by what Lantho said, because it had not occurred to him before that anyone could criticise Jedediah Spitalhouse except for the one thing he could not help having, a richly unusual name.

"No, it wasn't him that sent you," said Lantho. "And I've nothing much against that old Stewart; he puts up with me, and there's not many that do." He stood up and rubbed his knees. "My legs have pins and needles," he said. "Give me a hand up."

Mason reached his hand down, and Lantho took it. Then Mason was down in the water and Lantho was at the top of the bank looking down calmly. "You slipped," he said, when Mason stood up. "How did you manage to do that?"

"I don't know," said Mason. Lantho reached down his hand in turn to help Mason up, but Mason preferred to climb out alone. He was not quite able to think that Lantho had put him in the water, but he knew it was possible to think it. Lantho now seemed to have recovered his ordinary spirits.

"That was a welcome way to spend the morning," he said. "Now I'll go and see how he framed without me." And he walked off, leaving Mason to stand on the mill road with a pool of water forming round him.

He was soaked entirely. The coolness was not unwelcome, and the collar, at least, had lost its hardness, without growing any bigger. He waited a little while and then followed Lantho up the mill road to the level crossing. The gates had closed,

26

because the engine came across the road to the points before going to the far end of the train for the journey back up the line. Lantho had gone across, however, and was now standing in the sunshine at the bottom of the street, just where Mason and Moira had stood before she crossed to the station.

Now Moira came out of the station yard. Before she came out the new car drove through, with only the chauffeur and Fräulein in it. After it were Moira and her mother, and after them Jedediah Spitalhouse. Lantho stood and stared at them all. They walked past him, but not up the street. They went along beside the railway line and to the dock at the foot of the Incline. Mason thought he would go that way too, because of the discomfort of walking uphill in trousers that were wet and clarped to his knee.

He did not like, in his state, to accompany the Spitalhouses. He stood a long time by the crossing at the bottom of the street, until he saw Jedediah putting his family into a truck that was about to ascend the Incline.

The truck on the Incline went up. He saw the three heads above the sides. He walked along, limping with both legs, he thought, and waited for the next truck to be going up. He saw the Spitalhouses stop the truck when they had reached the level of their house by waving to the brakeman at the top of the Incline. They climbed out and waved again, and the empty truck went on, and down at the bottom the full one from the quarry came into the dock.

It was unhooked, and an empty one put in its place. Mason climbed aboard it, and waited for it to go. Steam rose from his clothes. With no warning but a wave the truck began to move and be lifted up the slope by the pull of the full one descending.

The full truck appeared at the far end and came down on exactly the same line, because there was only a single track and a passing place. Then, at the middle, Mason's truck swung to the left and the full one swung to the right, they drew abreast, and a quarryman taking a ride down shouted across to him, and Mason shouted back.

There was another shout too, and that was from Jedediah Spitalhouse, who was standing inside his own grounds over-looking the Incline. He was shouting at the man riding down on the load of stone. Passengers were meant to use only empty wagons and never loaded ones. The quarryman waved back to Jedediah's shout and turned his face away, hoping that he was not recognised.

Jedediah waved to Mason, and Mason waved back. Moira was there too, and waved her hat.

The wagon came up the last and steepest slope of the Incline and into the quarry top siding. The steel cable slacked itself and lay on the wooden rollers. The big wheel in the wheelhouse stopped moving and the brake blocks closed on its rim. The wagon wheels were scotched as it ran back towards the slope, and the rope was unhitched from it. A horse led the wagon away and another brought a full one back to the end of the cable. Mason stayed in the empty wagon, since he was already in it and usually no rides were allowed inside the quarry itself. The wagon did not go anywhere useful, but was put aside with others in front of the quarry smithy. Mason climbed out, and walked across the lines, round the buildings, and to the house.

He had forgotten by now that he was wet, but Mam noticed at once, and wanted to know how it had come about, and what he thought he had been doing, and what did he think clothes were for?

"I've had enough examinations," he said, "and I didn't do it on purpose."

"No, of course," said Mam. "But it wasn't what I expected you to do. How did you manage it?"

"I was helping a man called Lantho up the river bank," said Mason.

"Marrick Lantho," said Mam. "Yes, well, that's a queer darking sort of fellow, and I daresay he dropped you in."

"I daresay he did," said Mason. "But I don't know."

"You don't know with Lantho," said Mam. "He's not been quite right in himself in a long time. He was the other one after the Irishwoman, and when Jedediah won him to it he was nearly mad. They took him in, you know, near Leeds, but they never kept him, they sent him out a bit strange and that's all. Mind, he was like it before, always a sly one, like they are from Dacre. He was a shot-firer in these very quarries at that time, but they came not to trust him with the powder, blasting the wrong things for a lark."

"I didn't know about him," said Mason. "But I knew there was someone else wanted the Irishwoman."

"That was Marrick Lantho," said Mam.

The Irishwoman was Mrs Spitalhouse, Moira's mother. She had married Jedediah in his simple days, when he was a plain quarryman. Now that he had bettered himself into riches and ownerships she lived away from home, coming at intervals to visit Moira, and seeing her at her own small house further up the railway line, down the dale. It was generally agreed that she would come back to Jedediah if he would give up all his money, somehow, and have none of his new things. It was agreed that she was unreasonable about the matter, and that she wasn't being fair to Jedediah or the one who had been his rival and who now turned out to be Marrick Lantho.

The quarry whistle went. It was half past twelve and time for a meal. Mam said that Mason was back at the right time, but she wasn't expecting him, and why was he back. Had Mr Stewart sent him home because he was soaked through?

Mason explained about the examinations and the long wait for Mr Stewart, and the trouble with the pen nib.

"Well, he wouldn't want you for the tab-end of the week," said Mam. "But we'll know tomorrow, and that's as good as working, is the sure prospect of it."

Then Dad came in, enquiring after the smell of puddings that had come through the office window as the morning went on.

III

EVERY MORNING AT seven, summer and winter, Mrs Ross opened all the windows of the house, waited for the day's blast to thud the air, and closed the windows again. On Sunday mornings it was often not necessary, because there was hardly ever blasting then. Closed windows could be cracked or even broken, pushed in and pulled out by the elastic air.

Mason was woken on Saturday by Mam, at seven, when she opened the window. It was a quiet but bright morning, clouds lying softly across the sky and sunlight in patches on the fields and hills. The summer air came warm through the window.

They waited for the clock to chime downstairs. It was an accurate signal, because Dad made the shot-firer agree his watch with it before he set off to the fuses each morning. This morning the clock chimed, Mam and Mason waited for the strike of seven to begin, and for the explosion to accompany it. They heard all seven strokes, and no blast.

"I'll leave the windows open," said Mam. "It's rained a bit in the night and there's no dust, and it's grandly warm. You get up now, Mason."

There was a shout outside, then a small explosion that could not be blasting, and another shout. Mam stood and listened for a moment. "I don't know what that was," she said. "But there's your Dad off to see."

They both heard the door of the office next door slam shut, and Dad hurrying off into the quarry talking urgently to someone else.

"Accident," said Mason.

"Aye, happen," said Mam. "They can take him in the office if anyone's hurt. But now shift your bed and let me into that cupboard; I'll want something to wrap him in at least, if there's a hurt."

Mason got out of bed and Mam went into the cupboard where all the linen and clothes were kept. She came out with the white bundle of clean rag and sheeting that she used for bandages and dressings. It was tied round with a strip of its own substance, the first ready bandage. Mam fingered the knot as she came out of the cupboard. She had gone into it with concern on her face for some hurt man. She came out from it with a competent, trained look that was more than an expression but went deeper than the skin round her eyes and mouth, which was where the concern had showed first. Now she walked across the room differently, as if she were back in the hospital where she had worked, and she went down the stairs taking with her a confident assumption that what she did next would be the exactly right thing, understood by the patient and by doctors who saw him later.

Mason dressed and went downstairs. It was a day on which he had neither to go to school nor work, so he wore what he liked, short grey trousers and a grey shirt.

Mam had gone out of the house, leaving the door open. Mason went to the door and looked out. His eye was led to the centre face of the quarry by Mam, standing in the foreground and herself watching the next indication of where to look, which was at a group of men coming down the side of a tip among the tumbled stone and shale, still restless through not having lain long where it had been cast. The men were carrying. Beyond them, nearer the face of the rock and further back than the top of the tip was one of the big travelling cranes, standing idle, with steam rising about it and smoke hanging round it. The smoke was not coming from its chimney and the steam not from its valve, but seemed to come from its side. Behind it the cliff of the workface stood up to the sky, with the moorland and a crag of wall rounding the bite.

Work was slowing in the rest of the quarry now. The big saws in the building opposite ceased their rasping, and steam fell out among the blocks of waiting stone as the pistons of that engine were slowed to a stop. The bellows at the smithy could be heard sighing for a time, and then they too stopped. The talking anxious voices of men began to be heard. One of the men ran ahead from the carrying group and into the main building. The hooter there began to sound the signal that meant alarm, shout after shout after shout going up into the sky and coming back from the far side of the valley in the intervals of its own self, at a higher pitch than when it went out. By relaxing his ears, which Mason did against the piercing qualities of the hooter itself, he heard the original note and its return coming back as a narrow wailing, alarming in itself even if it did not already mean alert.

Then the wailing stopped, and a dense deafened silence came on Mason. The group coming from the steam crane came closer, and then, when it was on the level ground, it began to move faster. Mam turned and came to the door of the office and waited there. She motioned with her head for Mason to go

33

indoors out of the way. She said something but Mason did not hear what it was. It was either to tell him that he was to keep out of the way, or to warn him that he did not want to see the victim any more closely. Mason went in, and did something useful to the kettle, moving it three inches off the fire, so that he could tell himself he was too occupied to look from the window when the men came by.

He heard them come. He heard their boot-irons and their clog-irons scrape the stone flags outside. Men went into the office and came out. He looked from the window and saw them cross the rails and go to sit on the dock edge beside the building. Behind them hung steam curtains.

By the next truck up the Incline came Dr Connaught. Mason saw him hurrying over the rails and heard him going into the office. When he went the injured man went with him, lying on a board now, and wrapped and strapped with white cloth.

Mam and Dad came out of the office. Dad went to the workings again, because nothing was happening now anywhere. Mam came into the house. She carried a shrunken white bundle, tied as it had been before, and a darkened one she carried straight through to the scullery and put in a covered bucket. Then she washed her hands.

"That's that," she said when she came back. "A nasty cut leg and probably a broken arm, nothing too far out of the way. He's gone off now to the village and they'll either put him on a company wagon to go by train to Harrogate, or they'll send the motor ambulance for him. You don't have to worry about him any more, Mason."

"I wasn't," said Mason. "I don't even know who it was."

"One of the lads that lodges at Beaverside," said Mam. "We've sent off to tell his landlady. I don't know his name."

There was a tap at the door. Mam opened it. Outside there was Peter Ward, standing on one foot at a time and hanging the other down to scrape the boot-toe on the flag, catching at a fossil ripple with the sparking iron.

"Well now, Peter," said Mrs Ross.

"Is he in?" said Peter. "Mr Ross?"

"He's out in the quarry," said Mam. "If you want him you have to come to the office during office hours, not to the house."

"I want to go home," said Peter, with a sudden desperate wail in his voice, so loud and clear that it echoed from the building opposite in a broken way. Then he began to cry. "I saw it," he said. "I was just by."

"Come in, quarryman," said Mam. "You won't have liked that, Peter. But I saw him next, and he wasn't hurt that bad, you know."

"He wasn't doing owt," said Peter. "He was stood there, like, and the engine blew up; we were pulling it away from the face for the shots to be fired."

"You feel worse about it than if it had been you," said Mam.

"Aye," said Peter. "That I do."

"And he wasn't even your friend," said Mam.

"No," said Peter. "Just a fellow. He was called Andy."

"He's still called Andy," said Mam. "Sit down there, lad, and sup some tea, and then if you want to be off for the day you can go down to the village with Mason. I'll tell Mr Ross."

Peter sniffed, and sucked up some hot tea. Mason ate his breakfast. The saws started up again in the workshop, and

35

trucks began moving again outside, with the horses drumming their slow solemn walk on the sleepers between the rails.

Dad came back before long. "I'll have my breakfast," he said. "Then I'll be out again. We've got trouble with that crane, and I want it sided up before Jedediah comes. They've sent him a message on by the railway telephone from the dock so he won't be so long."

He ate his breakfast hurriedly, with one eye at the window all the time in case he was wanted. "You've poured this tea hot, Mother," he said, putting it down and pouring more milk in it. "Cut me a bit of bread, Mason."

"Peter wants to be off now," said Mason. "He was next to the one that got hurt."

"Aye," said Dad, looking at Peter but not really thinking of him, only of the crane up on the tip. "He'll loss his money that's all, but there's nowt for him to be doing today."

Dad went out, chewing a huge mouthful of bread and bacon. Then he came back and said that they would be blowing the shots as soon as they had the crane out of the way, and there wouldn't be any warning.

Mam told Mason and Peter to be off as soon as they could. Peter was to check in at the office before going off work. Mason was to take the shopping list down to the village and bring back what had been ordered. Mam herself was going to tidy up a bit for Jedediah.

They went down the lane, where the copper butterflies were few and slow on this duller day. The butterflies were silent in the air, and both boys were silent with them. They came out beyond where the butterflies were, to the place where they could look across the broad growing meadow-field to the

Incline. A wagon was going down. Beyond it, among the tree-tops, showed the chimneys of Jedediah's new house.

"Do you see her oft," said Peter. "I mean visiting, and like that?"

"The Irishwoman?" said Mason. "I ken her, she kens me."

"Never mind the Irishwoman," said Peter. "She's nowt to anyone but Jed. I mean the lass, Myra."

"Moira," said Mason. "She'll never be owt to any of us, she's been reared different."

"Happen," said Peter. "But she's the same breed when all's said, and a bonny little heifer."

"And we're lads out of the quarry," said Mason.

"Aye," said Peter. "And we'll mak' do, and never addle the right brass for all we'd like."

"I've addled nowt yet," said Mason. "I'll mebbe not get taken on."

"Aye, there's me in trade and thee in business," said Peter. "And with our first brass we'll do what quarry lads do of a Saturday."

"Aye, we'll that," said Mason. But he was not sure what it was to be.

"Aye," said Peter. "We'll be away to the Nanny Goat Inn and get sick with ale and hear the sermon o' Sunday like men—with headaches."

The Nanny Goat Inn was an Inn up on the moors above the quarry. It was famous for cock-fighting, gambling, bad beer, and a drink brewed on the premises called heather ale.

"We'll have to do that, then," said Mason. "Can I if I get taken on at the bank?" He hoped Peter would say No, that it was contrary to accepted practice.

"You can, right enough," said Peter. "They say Lantho gets there one time and another and tells all what the grand folks have in their banks, but the directors don't hear it."

"Him that was mad for the Irishwoman," said Mason.

"Him," said Peter.

The lane sank into a cutting of its own, and the walls rose high enough to block any view of the Incline and the house beyond. Before they went down with it lower than the fields Mason saw Moira riding a horse in those far grounds. He was filled with a gladness he had begun to recognise but not to understand or expect. He was always gladder to see Moira than to see anyone else. Jedediah had for a long time been a special hero to him, and to Mam and Dad, partly for what he had done for them, and partly for what he had achieved for himself with only the same background and bringing up. He was the wealthiest person any of them knew, indeed the only wealthy person, yet he was approachably the same man that Dad had been to school with. He had not become inaccessible or proud. And it was understood that the way he was bringing Moira up was right, and wealth would give her opportunity to enter a wider world than that of quarrying and farming, and the same wealth, properly applied to paying people like Fräulein, would give Moira the manners and customs to go with the inheritance. So Jedediah had not changed his nature as an equal man to Mr Ross, and had not altered his kind by belonging to the species of rich men. No one in the Ross house believed that Jedediah could be criticised, except a little about the Irishwoman. Now, though, without thinking any less of Jedediah, Mason only saw him as a sign that Moira might be somewhere near, and was disappointed if she had not come with him.

"Jed's coming," said Peter. Mason thought Peter had mistaken Moira for her father, but Peter had been looking the other way, to where the road, rather than the lane, came along the hill from the East, having climbed a roundabout way to the same elevation. Peter had seen a flash of sunlight on paint or glass, where Jedediah's car had turned along from the highway on to the quarry road.

Mason came back alone from the village, dragging the shopping to the foot of the Incline and going up when a truck came for the dock. He went up with the last load of the day, the men at the bottom said. They were wanting to know why it was the last load, but Mason hardly knew about the quarry business. He went up without wondering about it any more, and watched the grounds beside the Incline for Moira. She did not show herself, but he had seen her once and was not discontented. All the same, even if he could not feel unhappy about not seeing her, he was aware of a hollow feeling about the rest of the day when he had come to the top of the Incline and got out of the truck. When he stopped moving the day itself seemed to stop.

Then it seemed to start again, but not for anything to do with Moira. As he came near to the house and office he heard that two or three separate rows were going on. A large group of men argued with the clerk who came on Saturdays to pay them, usually in the evening. Now they were being paid in the middle of the day, several hours of work short. The clerk, who was small and old, went on handing out money to man after man, and the men went on arguing with him about the unfairness of it, and demanding full money because it was not their fault they were being sent off early.

Another group was arguing because the men in it expected to

leave in the middle of the day but were being made to stay. They were the smithy men and engineers, and they had the steam crane to manage and put right. It had still not been moved away from the quarry face. This group argued inside itself, but the man who didn't mind staying at work was big Bucko Robinson, the smith himself, and without him on their side the others could not unite.

Two more men were arguing with Mrs Ross. All the groups were outside the house and the office and she had naturally been drawn in, or out, and was telling these two, the shot-firer and his mate, that they could not go away without firing the shots, because of the danger of leaving the charges of powder about. But the shots could not be fired until the crane had been moved, and it had come off its rails.

In the office itself the worst argument was raging. The outside noise grew less and less as the men left, going down the Incline in full truckloads. The laid-off workers went first, then the smiths and engineers to get their dinners at home. The shot-firer and his mate ran out of explosive remarks to make.

Mr Ross and Jedediah Spitalhouse were shouting in the office. Mason had not heard Jedediah scold Dad before. He could hear that a great deal of blame was being cast about by Jedediah, who was saying such things as: "Nobody said you were an engineer, but you know enough to get a machine mended before it breaks," and: "You've had the money, man, you've had the bloody money, look, here's the bloody account; so why hasn't the work been done?" and: "That sort of thinking's no good in business, Ross, so don't think it at me. I'm dealing with facts. You've failed me, and you've failed the lads

40

outside, there's no work for them until you get yourself sided up and sorted up."

After some more of the shouting Jedediah came out of the office, looked at the remaining men, said "Right lads, you know what you've to be doing, and the sooner the better," opened the door of his car, climbed in, slammed the door, shouted at the driver to drive home, and then shouted at him for being half out of the car instead of driving when he had only been getting out to open the door for Jedediah. They drove away.

Dad came out of the office and straight into the house. Mam nodded her head to Mason, who had been waiting on the dock and watching, and he came in after her.

"It's not right," Dad was saying. "I won't be tret like that. He's come out above himself, when he's no better than ordinary folk. He's mebbe the boss of me in money, but he isn't boss of me as a man, and by God I'll be down here after and set him to rights with one hand as I am. Of course I know about his damn machines, but what can I do when there's no money comes, and no parts either, for all he points to papers and says it's there. I've not had it, or them, and what there was of spares got taken years ago, and I'd prove that if I had the papers, but you know who has the papers, Mr Holier-than-Ross Spitalhouse, director of this company. I'm not a paper man; I do it in spite of the papers, but he won't give me a paper man, so who's he to wonder if they aren't clerked like railway tickets? I'm not doing anything different, so why hasn't he found it wrong before? He's been in the trade as long as I have. Why am I different all of a sudden?"

"You want your dinner," said Mam.

41

"Do I hell," said Dad. "I'm off to see that crane." And he walked out of the house, throwing down the papers he had brought in with him.

"We'll have ours," said Mam.

"Good," said Mason. "I mean, I haven't stopped being hungry because of anything else."

"No," said Mam. "I think I have. I don't know what's come over Jedediah. I've not known him like this before. You know he's done well for this quarry and the town, because they go together, and the accounts don't show a big profit for him and the other directors. He makes his money in other places, so this spot isn't much to him. Perhaps he just thinks of it as a little place, and he was always easiest to cross in small ways. I mean, when the Irishwoman left him the first time, when Moira was only a little thing, he was more bothered that she'd hired a trap to the station instead of taking his own that was to cost him no more. But he was bothered that time, for her leaving. We saw him a lot, and little Moira stopped here a month or more."

"I don't remember," said Mason. "When?"

"You don't need to be embarrassed," said Mam. "You were three, and she was two and something."

But Mason was not embarrassed. He was excited to think that he had so much historical intimacy with Moira as that, and annoyed that he could remember nothing about it and had not known before.

"Eat up," said Mam. "There's plenty. And you wait; Jedediah Spitalhouse will side up, or else."

IV

THE QUARRY WAS empty in the afternoon, except for one centre of activity, the only place that drew men and animals to it, the crane. To it had gone during the morning the eight horses that worked there, and the men who were engineers and smiths. In the afternoon the men came back, and the horses had not left but eaten hay as they stood in their gear.

Mason went up the tips after his dinner to see what was going on. The crane had come off its rails. It was the big crane, capable of lifting ten ton blocks of stone, and often used for lifting bigger ones than that if necessary. To be able to lift ten tons at the jib the crane itself had to weigh more than that, to balance itself. Part of the weight was its own structure, thick strong steel, and part was stone laid on the back platform. When the crane had burst its cylinder-head, the resulting overthrow of the piston rod, jamming the piston on the broken metal, had pulled the driving axle up into the frame and drawn one pair of wheels off the rails. There had been a lot of movement of metal parts that should not have moved, and a great splintering of wooden decking, and a burning of it too when the fire had been raked out at once on to the track to lessen the amount of steam and hot water. The fire had had to come out because steam pipes had burst and a pressure core melted and there was no water left in the boiler.

43

Now the crane was a hot derelict, crooked on its ten-foot gauge track, and men and horses toiled round it. Mr Ross was not much help there. Everybody knew what had to be done, and the best helpers were the strongest ones. Mr Ross had only one hand to help with, and had not the strength in his shoulders now to push even with them and be effective. He stayed for some time, and then was displaced by a brawny engineer, and gave up physical help. There was no overseeing to be done that needed authority, so he left the scene and went home.

Mason was sitting on a rejected stone by the path he took towards the house. "Best be away back," said Dad. "There's still shots in that face waiting to be fired."

"I'll come home then," said Mason. "I thought the shot-firer was having to take them out again."

"Not if he doesn't have to," said Dad. "You can't get them out clean, and it's risky work; he might just chance on a spark. No, he's staying by to fire them off if he gets a chance. But we've to get the crane free if we can. What a mess, eh? That might have killed somebody, an accident like that, or scalded them, and that's worse, mebbe."

He had recovered his temper now. Jedediah's words were further off and not still ringing against his ears, but they were not forgotten. After his late dinner Dad went into the office again and searched the papers there, without being able to find quite what he wanted. He was still looking at tea time, and came out when he heard the horses coming down off the tip and the men coming by. He had forgotten the immediate problem of the crane while he searched for something to justify his way of having run things. He came out with papers under his arm, blowing the stone dust from them. He was offering to pay the men who had been working, but they said no, they didn't want anything until they had done the job, and so far they had not succeeded. Big Bucko Robinson said they weren't wanting any ale-money tonight, they'd be back in the morning and get the crane on its tracks and shifted in some manner or another. "We can mannish," he said, "but I doubt it's a weary task."

"Well, I'm sorry, lads," said Dad.

"That engine should mebbe have been fettled long syne," said Bucko. "It could have struck more than one man. But we'll be back first thing and make a teagle and lift it wi' that."

A teagle is a three-legged support for the pulley or block, and the quarrymen were always building them about the place to lift blocks of stone on to trucks and lorries, in places where the cranes could not be brought because there was no track. The men were not meant to use them since they were probably only used once and were not strongly made and too many accidents happened. Dad's accident was caused by the slipping of the leg of a teagle and the snapping of a chain.

The men went off, walking down the Incline, where no trucks were running this evening. Dad went back to the office and looked through papers again, and came late to his tea.

"I just can't lay hands on it," he said, when he did come in. "And when I do I'll take it straight to Jedediah and show him."

"Well, you know what it is and we don't," said Mam. "So you'll mebbe know what he'll say."

"You never know quite that with Jedediah," said Dad. "I never thought to hear him like he was this morning. But I'm looking for the directors' instructions to me about the engineers' report on the equipment. You know they have it all looked to each six months, and a report goes to the directors. Well, I don't see that, but I get told what to do, and I want to find the instructions, because I know there's not a word about that crane, or any other steam engine, except repacking the glands and greasing. When I can show that to Jedediah I'll know I'm right, and so will he."

"They didn't tell you what to do," said Mason. "They forgot, or something."

"They forgot, or something," said Dad. "I'm wondering what else Jedediah has forgotten; there's things that come to mind, like not having any instructions about those cranes for three years, when before they used to have some new part on every few months. But now there's not anything in the smithy for them, not even a bit of tow for packing, and the running-gear, the ropes of the jibs and so on, haven't been renewed or touched for a couple of years."

"Aye," said Mam, "and who's getting the blame? You are; and him it belongs to, him that orders or doesn't order, he's stood behind you in his grand house with his grand governesses and motors and stuck-up little princess, and all going his way."

"He has his brass," said Dad, "and his motor, and all, but he hasn't his Irishwoman. But I've got my grand sensible Yorkshire lass, and I can manage with that if there's nowt else." He leaned across the tea table and embraced Mam with his good arm.

"Eh now, behave," said Mam, straightening the tablecloth with her hands; "you're spilling the tea, and making our lad blush."

"Hold still," said Dad, leaning over still harder and giving her a kiss over one eye and another on her chin. "Let him blush."

Mason was blushing more at the mention of Moira as Jedediah's princess. He wanted to get up and say that she was not a princess, or not at all to blame for anything her father had made her, and that besides anything they thought she was or had been, he thought she had a special relationship to his world. But there was no way of saying anything that would describe feelings that he did not know how to feel or ideas he did not know how to think. He had finished his tea, so he got up and went outside.

At the top of the Incline he stood and looked at the valley. There was Green Hill straight opposite, with the town at its foot; and a little apart from the town, a little apart from the ordinary world, the other side of the Incline stretched like some sword between it and the commonplace, was Moira's house, Bishopside Hall. He saw only the roof of it among still trees. He leaned against the blocks at the end of a siding, and waited for something to happen in the misty overhung evening, for some revelation of the world to come out of the trees, for some settling of the swell of emotion that washed over him when he saw Moira or the house, or, to some extent, Jedediah. Why, he wondered, did such fascination exist for another person? Why did it come so unbidden, so strong, and why could it be so often absent if it were real? And what was it? No answer came out of the evening. And then Bishopside Hall was once more a glimpse of roof among trees, small in the world and not the whole of it or its centre.

There was a noise in the quiet sidings behind him. He turned away from the valley and looked to see what was happening, why there was a dull spluttering. Among the rust-flanked rails with their polished tops there was the spluttering thing, long and thin and moving, writhing. Mason stood startled for a time, and then knew what it was. But his heart banged and beat faster before he realised. By the smithy stood the shot-firer, who had thrown among the rails the lengths of fuse he had laid for the morning's shots. Fuse is delicate stuff and can only be laid once, and ought not to be left lying about if it has been discarded. He had brought the pieces here, where the ground was open, and lit them from the smithy fire and was watching them splutter themselves from end to end among the rails.

Mason walked over to him, and smelt the sharp smell of the burning, and stood with his back to the warm smithy doorway and its furnace of fallen fire.

"Best be rid of what you can't make nowt of," said the shot-firer. "Then we'll be off home, tell your Dad. I don't want to be at the trouble of walking over there." Then he spat at the last yards of burning fuse, missed all the self-destroying sparks, and walked off to the Incline. Mason decided he had not been very friendly. The shot-firer's mate came over the tracks from the quarry, where he had been locking the powder store, without a word threw the key to Mason, and followed the shot-firer. Mason watched them go, and took the key home. The last sparks died to fallen ash among the ballast and rails. The quarry was entirely still now.

In the morning the smiths and engineers walked up the Incline and were at work very early in a slight drizzle. They were dragging some very large timbers up to make the teagle. There was nothing for Dad to do there. He spent part of the morning in the office, unable to find the papers he wanted, and then went down, as usual, with Mam and Mason to church for the morning service.

Moira was often but not always at church in the morning. This morning Mason did not see her before or during the service, and did not think of her. Mam had wondered whether Jedediah would come, whether he dared face the people now that his company had had to send some of the men home with short wages. The Spitalhouses sat at the front of the church on the days they were there. Today their seats were empty. Mam whispered to Dad that there was a reason for it.

Jedediah and Moira had come in late and sat at the back. Far from being shunned when, after the service, people talked to each other on the way out, Jedediah was spoken to by a number of people. But Dad was only nodded to by the same people, and he and Jedediah did not let their eyes meet.

"Well," said Mam huffily, even in church, "that's all the wrong way round: that man's to blame, not us, and no one spoke to me at all."

Mason saw Moira, but looked away again, because she was all at once on the other side from his own family, in another unfriendly camp, and to allow any response inside himself would be traitorous. He felt a pain and a turning in his chest, and his breath came shallow and his head swam: the more he resisted the undefined attraction that Moira had for him the stronger it became, until outside, in the churchyard, it went, when Mam asked him whether he was all right. And by then he was, and was hoping that Jedediah's motor was outside so that he could look more closely at it.

It was not there, and the only disappointment he felt was a mechanical one.

49

"We'll be off and see how that teagle's going," said Dad. "If Spitalhouse wants me he can come up; I'm not standing here for him."

The teagle was up, with two sheaves on the rope, so that there was a reduction gear. If the horses pulled a yard of rope the crane axle would be lifted two inches, making it possible for great weights to be lifted. Great things can be moved in small pieces. The crane had been lifted up and propped and work was going on to restore the axle. The smithy fires were roaring hot and red and metal was laid in it to soften and be re-shaped. The black bellows behind the fires sucked and pressed and the leather flaps across their openings fluttered and rattled between being open and shut.

"We're winning," said Bucko Robinson to Mason, pulling on one of the bellows beams and squirting air into the coals, then relaxing as his mate pulled the other beam down and lifted Bucko's ready for the next stroke.

After dinner the smithy was still full of bellow-breathing and the beating of metal. Mason watched for a while, but he was not useful and the smiths were too busy working to talk even among themselves. Mason had nothing to do for the afternoon, and went back home to see whether anything was happening apart from the ceaseless enquiry that Mam had begun about the behaviour of each person she knew and why they had not spoken to her at church. Dad listened for a time, and did his own joining in, then slept a little, and then went to see how the crane was being mended.

He went out of the front door, because that was the convenient side. They had only used the back door so far that day. Under the weatherboard, at the foot of the door, something rustled. It was an envelope addressed to Mason Ross.

"Postman's been," said Dad. In those days there was a Sunday post.

Mason took the letter and opened it. Inside there was a single sheet, headed Vendale Savings Bank, and saying that the position of clerical assistant was offered to him, at a yearly rate that sounded a lot to Mason until Dad rapidly turned it into shillings a week, when it was not much. He was to start the next day at eight thirty at the branch in the village.

"Do they have others?" said Mason, surprised by the thought.

"Plenty," said Dad. "Mebbe you'll get to be manager of one of them." He was pleased, and thumped Mason on the back with the stump of his left wrist in his pleasure, hurting himself.

"In business," said Mam. "Well, I am that pleased."

Mason was pleased too, and went out for a walk. Now he needed no object for the day. He had tomorrow's work to think of; another day was to be added to the list of extraordinary days. He went up behind the quarries, along the moorland to a sandy road that stretched along the top of the hill to give access to fields and pastures. He turned along the road, away from the only building on it, the small cottage called the Nanny Goat Inn, and towards the woodland beyond the quarry end. Far up the road, by the Inn, two or three quarrymen stood in the road or lay in the grass by its verge. Next Sunday, perhaps, he thought, he and Peter Ward would take their money there and be initiated into the mysteries of getting sick on ale, part of working for a living. There was a problem about what Mam would say or Dad would do, but perhaps being a working, or business, man would solve that.

Mason felt that half life was behind him now, half its difficulties over, half its terrors spent. And now he had the new armour of his own independence to shield him. If you can earn your own living from the world then you can exist somehow independent of it as well. Mason looked about him to see what the world was, and how it related to him. To the left the fields went down six hundred feet to the river above the village; to the right was the little wood, which was where he felt like walking, his own private place.

He climbed the wall and went in on the pine needles. The low sky rested in the tops of the trees. Occasional drops from the morning's drizzle gathered and fell, so that there were darker places where the natural arrangements of branches made natural gutters. There was plenty of dry, though, and better than that was the sparse growing of raspberry bushes with small new fruit hardening but not yet red. One was slightly pink and he ate it. It was sharp and hairy among his teeth.

At the foot of a bush he found the white gleaming bones of a long-dead rabbit, clean and fresh and distinct but fallen apart, dry in the dustless pine needles. He looked and looked and fingered the skull and stroked the bones of leg and hip and back, and knew, in a moment of understanding everything in the world, how they had joined together and been a living creature. Understanding that meant that he understood the whole world. Then the frame that held the thought jarred and the understood picture broke into unrelated parts; the skeleton was scattered by time again. But he had understood it, and had known it. He sat and tried to recover it, but all his thoughts slipped, as if he had forgotten how to think.

Then someone called to him, and he knew he could never understand anything, there was no knowledge. Moira was in the road on her pony, and had seen him over the wall.

"What are you doing?" she said. "I haven't anything to do. I've run away from nasty stupid Fräulein. Well, she isn't nasty or stupid, but I am, and nothing ever happens and Mummy's gone again and Daddy's in a black mood. He has business worries, you know."

"I know," said Mason. "I'm a business man too." He told her about the letter from Mr Stewart, and would have shown it to her if he had not left it at home. "I've left school," he said.

"I've never been to school," said Moira. "Just Fräuleins and joining in other people's classes in Harrogate. But they laugh at me in Harrogate because I talk broader Yorkshire than they do, and they laugh at me here because they think I'm putting an airs, so there isn't anyone for a friend. Who's your friend, Mason?"

Mason thought that at the moment a dead rabbit was his most useful close friend, but when he wondered how to express himself the image and memory and understanding went away, and he could think of no friend at all. "I don't know," he said.

"Nor do I," said Moira. "But you'll find some more at the Bank, I expect. Daddy will know people. I wish I could go and work. If I went to school I could leave next term and go into one of the mills like Mummy. But Daddy's so rich it would be a silly thing to do. I can't work and I haven't anyone to play with. Fräulein doesn't think any of the village girls are suitable, and the ones I know in other places don't want to play. They've stopped playing. I know, we'll go to my house and play in the nursery. Do you remember when we used to play when we were little. I threw wooden bricks at you once."

Then Mason realised that it was Moira who was standing the other side of the wall from him, that it was Moira who had once been the little girl he had played with in her nursery, but that the little girl and the little boy he must have been once were different now, although they sprang from those earlier selves. He did not want to play with bricks, or the imagining games of childhood, or the more recent and conversational pastimes of Snakes-and-Ladders or Ludo. He did not want to play anything. He was content to be one side of a wall, in possession of his own world of spinney and rabbit bone and possible raspberries. But this was the new Moira of the last few weeks, who had stopped being a mere acquaintance, a mere friend, most of the time, and had become something else, not to the rest of the world but to him.

He looked at her, and she was looking up at the trees, not at him.

"I love you," he said.

"Do you?" said Moira. "I don't love you. At least, not as much as I love Fräulein when she's good and doesn't smell of camphor. She smells of camphor on Sundays. If you come to the house you'll see."

Mason had surprised himself with what he said. He had not known what he meant until it was words. And now he knew that Moira did not know what he meant either. As well as that, he did not know what she meant. "What's camphor?" he said, because there is nothing to add to 'I love you', yet something has to be said.

"German stuff," said Moira. "It smells like macaroons. You come and smell Fräulein now, because I haven't anyone else to play with."

Mason came over the wall. He now began to realise that he had on his Sunday and business suit, with the high biting collar. The new crease that Mam had steamed into the trousers was being lost by walking and kneeling. Pine needles were in the turn-up of the trouser legs and there was a mark of green wall on one sleeve.

"You look hot," said Moira. But it was not hotness that had come to redden Mason's face. It was shame of having said something so personal to Moira and not being understood, the pity of spoiling a day by saying what he had and understanding what he meant; by understanding and naming his feelings he had destroyed the nervous quality of them. They were labelled now, or it was labelled now, and displayed to him as something smaller and less worth having than he had expected; as if he had pulled out the middle of a flower in a search for nectar and found the nectar soured by the juice of the flower itself.

"I'm daft," he said, hoping that such an admission would take away anything he had said, from Moira's memory and from his.

"Happen," said Moira, in just Jedediah's voice and tone, and they both laughed at it and tried to say it to each other without managing again that hint of gravel at the bottom of Jedediah's voice.

Attempting his voice reminded Mason of the previous morning. "Did your Dad say owt about they had a quarrel him and my Dad?" he asked.

"I haven't seen him to talk to," said Moira. "He's always

doing his papers. But they wouldn't have a quarrel; they're friends."

"My Dad thinks they did," said Mason.

"That's them," said Moira. "We don't have to bother. Now you'll have to run a bit to keep up because the horse wants to go quicker, and if I get home first I'll wait for you at the gate. Come along."

The way was downhill on a gravelly road with ruts where quarry carts had been up and down full and empty. Mason ran part of the way as fast as he could and then jogged the rest because he could not keep up with the horse. At one place, out of breath and terribly hot, he almost climbed the wall and went home. But he went on down and down and came dusty to the gate of Bishopside Hall.

Moira was not waiting at the gate. He stood a moment and wondered whether to go past. Then he went in a little way up the drive. He saw Moira at an upstairs window, having some garment pulled over her head by Fräulein. He waited then by the front door. The woodpigeons purred in the trees round him. A door banged in the house, a voice sounded, and Moira came out, wearing now a white dress and brushing her hair, calling back to Fräulein that it didn't matter about Mason, he could see her brushing, he isn't a visitor, I just know him.

The nursery was a room Mason had known since it was built. He had a memory of it without a roof and full of light. Now that the roof was on the light came green through the trees and made a mid-afternoon dusk. Later on in the day, he knew, sunlight would come from the west.

"So dark," said Moira. "Dowly," because she could speak

Yorkshire well enough in spite of elocution in Harrogate and elegant manners taught elsewhere. Now she clambered up on to the broad window bottom and became a shape, her white dress being a solidity against the green outside.

"I don't know what to do," she said. "If I stand up and jump off here will you catch me?"

"If you like," said Mason. He stood ready, but she got to her feet and sat down again, not daring to jump.

"Get me Betty and Loosan," she said.

"I don't know about dolls," said Mason.

"You must know," said Moira, "or you wouldn't know they were. You know where they are."

Mason knew. He knew the cupboard and he knew the dolls by name, but he was not pleased to know; it was knowledge he was ashamed of. He got out Betty with her hard body and Loosan with her stuff sawdust-filled one. He handed them up to Moira. They were beginning to smell old, he thought, unwashed, their sweetness decayed.

"Minta, Florence," said Moira, when she had sat the first two on the window bottom with her. Mason handed them up, knowing each one and hating to do so. Dolls did not interest him, and these were not new to him at all but, like their smell, a little stale. They went through them all, Daisy, Jecka, Hildy, Lorly, except for a bundle of little ones she did want to be troubled with.

"Lessons," she said. "We are having lessons. Children sit up, and Mister Fräulein will tell you your lessons. Teach them something, Mason."

"No," said Mason, sitting on the floor. From here it seemed to him that nine dolls sat against the window and that nothing he knew could be taught to them. "I don't want to play," he said, "any more. I work now; I go to business."

"Help me down," said Moira, holding out one hand for him to take and jerking herself on to the floor. "You can let go of my hand now, Mason. Now bring them all back to the cupboard and we'll put them away."

Mason obeyed again, and brought the dolls one by one and they were laid out on the shelf. "I don't think I want dolls any more," said Moira. "They won't play with me any more. It's not the same as it was." She brought Loosan out of the cupboard again and squeezed the sawdust-filled body. "I'm sure she's got money, or messages, inside," she said. "Shall we cut her open?" She pulled off Loosan's dress, and showed the clean cloth body under it, with dirty marks of use down as far as the neckline and beyond the sleeve ends.

"No," said Mason, because he knew it was unfair and improper and that there was no money, no message, inside Loosan.

"She's only a French doll, from when I had Mam'zell," said Moira. "That was a long time ago. And she's very stupid and won't learn English."

"I don't want to play with dolls any sort of way," said Mason.

"This isn't playing," said Moira. She put the doll into his hands and went to the little inlaid box that held sewing things. She came back with a small pair of pointed scissors. "Look," she said, opening the scissors and jabbing one of the blades into Loosan's heart. Loosan groaned in her heart. "Oh dear," said Moira, looking away from her victim and at Mason. She smiled partly in enjoyment, partly in guilt at committing a murder, and partly as Mason's accomplice.

58

"I'm not doing it," said Mason. Moira closed the scissors and made an incision, then pulled the scissors out. The cloth over the heart stayed shut and the incision hardly showed. Moira looked at her own creased skin on finger and thumb. "You finish it," she said. "It's terribly hard."

Mason took Loosan and the scissors and completed the cut halfway round Loosan's body. Sawdust began to spill out.

"Dead, dead, dead," said Moira. "Oh, Loosan." But there was no turning back now. She took Loosan and opened her like an egg so that her contents ran out on the shelf. There was sawdust. There was nothing else. Loosan had died for nothing.

Then Fräulein had come in, and to them as they stood by the cupboard looking at the evidence of playful murder.

"Goodtness, Anglisch children breaking," she said. "But it is de same in Yarmany."

"We didn't mean to, quite," said Moira.

"That too is de same in Yarmany," said Fräulein. Mason could smell the strong smell that Moira had mentioned for Sunday. It was somehow like paraffin, he thought. He wondered whether Fräulein had a bad cold, because he was reminded of some cold-cure. Fräulein had taken the dying Loosan from the shelf and looked at her hollow body, and run her fingers through the sawdust. "It is liver and lungcks and heart and stomagg," she said. "I will put them back. I have been noorse in hospital."

"Oh Fräulein," said Moira, "nobody else cares." She laid her head against Fräulein and put her arms half round her.

"These poor sick Puppe," said Fräulein, "we shall sew cured. Now it is time for tea, and your friend will have to go."

"Oh, Mason, I do like you," said Moira. But she did not look at him because she was gathering up the spilt sawdust in her hands and carrying it across the nursery, following Fräulein. Mason followed her, and when they came to the side door, leading towards the Incline, he said Goodbye. Moira turned towards him and touched him on his elbow with her elbow, smiled, lifted her hands towards her face, and blew sawdust into his eyes. When he could see again Moira and Fräulein had gone, and he went out through the door and across the grounds to the gate by the Incline.

The Incline was empty. The wire cable lay slackened along the rails, because the wagon at the bottom was against a stop and the wagon at the top was pulled close to the big wheel and there was no tension. Mason crossed the cable carefully, since it could have tautened and lifted itself up suddenly and thrown him over. It did not move.

At home only Mam was there. During the afternoon the smiths and engineers had moved the damaged crane well away from the work-face, and now Dad had gone down to the village for the shot-firers, to get the shots blown tonight and the danger finished with. It was always possible for someone to come by and drop the end of a cigarette into one of the shotholes and be blown up. And only the shot-firers knew exactly where the explosives had been put.

"Where have you been?" Mam asked.

"Just a walk," said Mason. "Thinking about tomorrow."

"Sawdust on you," said Mam, brushing him. "That's tomorrow's suit, Mason. How did you get that?" But before he could answer her she found a long dark hair on his sleeve and then another by his collar. "Have you been down to Spitalhouses?" she said.

"Yes," he said.

Mam dropped the hairs into the fire. "You'd no call to be going there," she said. "What are you thinking of? You should have more sense than that; after what he said to your father, how he's treated him in front of the men, you shouldn't want to go there. We've been mistaken about Jedediah all these years. We thought there was generosity and friendship in that man, but there isn't. All he's done for us is done for himself, that's what, and when there comes any difficulty he won't support us. So you can stop away from that house: you don't live your own life yet, Mason Ross; you live here. Well, I'll say nothing to your father, but don't do it again."

There were sausages for tea. Mason pierced the skin of his and the inside welled out. "It is liver and lungs and heart and stomach," he said.

"Don't play with your food," said Mam. "You're too old for that."

V

MASON WAS LYING in bed next morning feeling rich, because of the working days that began for him now, when Mam came in and opened the window. The clock struck. Nothing happened. There was no blasting in the quarry. Dad had been down the night before to look for the shot-firer but had not found him.

"Shot-firer thinks it's Sunday yet," said Mam. "But up here it's Monday."

"Work," said Mason.

"That's it," said Mam, and she laid him a new hard collar on the bed and left him. Mason came to breakfast later choked so tight he thought he would not be able to eat. Dad came through from the office muttering that he had not much time, the shot-firer would be down any minute to say whether he could fire or not, and then they would have to see about what men could work. If there was unfired explosive in the face of the quarry then the men would have to stay out of that piece.

The shot-firer came soon. Dad went out to talk with him. Mason and Mam listened to what was being said. The shot-firer was being indignant because he said Dad had shifted the shots, and Dad was being indignant because he said that the shot-firer had forgotten where the shots had been put. Dad came in again, still muttering about how the day's work could be organised, and he didn't want to send men off with no work.

When Mason left the house Dad was up on the face with the shot-firer, helping him dig with a wooden spade. Mason thought suddenly that he would rather be up there with them, digging and moving the living earth, than in a dry wall-bounded office adding up numbers and turning them into miles and furlongs or hundredweights, quarters, stones and pounds. He had often thought the same thing on the way to school, and it had been easier to forget then, because as soon as he got to the school gate there would be somebody with some new idea, some new fight, ready. Today it would all be new. But he could not tell that it would be interesting.

Butterflies flew from his path. He thought he heard their wings. Then he thought the noise might have been the rope of the Incline, pulling taut as a truck was brought full to the top. He could see the rope vibrating, first in waves and then in a blur that made it invisible for itself and hid what was behind it. By the time he got to the bottom of the lane there was a truck descending, and he heard its axle groaning.

He saw other boys who were going to school still. He wanted to turn down the road with them and into that gate; he knew what went on in school, but he did not know what went on in Banks.

Then he found he was too late to go to school ever again. As he passed Church Cottages a small fat child walked out into his way from a doorstep. He stopped, and the child stopped. Its mother came to the door, took it by the hand and said "Out of the master's way." So Mason knew he was no longer a school boy but a consequential clerk.

He heard the train come in as he entered the High Street. He came to the door of the bank at exactly the same time as Lantho, who came up unsmiling and gaunt, yellowish and aloof, from the station. Mason could not help smiling, pleased at being here on time, but Lantho did not smile. He opened the door of the Bank and went in without saying anything.

"Have that desk," he said at last. "Boy."

"Yes," said Mason. Then he said "Sir," to be on the polite side of things.

"I'm not going to tell you where anything is," said Lantho. "If it's wanted you'll have to find it for yourself. But you'd better begin by making a fair copy of the lists on your desk."

Mason found several sheets of paper with words and figures on them, and another sheet, lined and ruled, for the copy. On the desk lay a feather, a bottle of ink, and a small box with sand in it. The feather was the pen he had to use, the ink was the ink, and the sand was, Lantho said, to blot neat work with. Mason began to copy. The first line went well. It was "Cheques outstanding and current". But the second line became a mess, because the soft point of the quill bent over and laid ink down instead of pounds.

"You have some bad pens here," said Mason. "That one I did my exam with wasn't a good runner, and this one's crossed."

"Get another," said Lantho. "I just thought I'd set you up right at the beginning, but if you can't use a real pen then you can't. But you have to get your day's work in, so find a pen sharpish, Boy."

Mason found a pen in the desk drawer, together with some real blotting paper. "I think you're tricking me," he said.

"Do your work," said Lantho, settling down to entries in his

64

big ledger. Mason went round next looking for a sheet of paper like the one he had messed up. Lantho did not mind where he looked. Mason set to work again.

Mr Stewart came in half an hour later. Lantho stood up when he did and sat straight down again. Mr Stewart said "Good morning", and went through to his own office. Mason wondered whether he ought to have stood up like Lantho, but Mr Stewart was through before he had made up his mind.

Mr Stewart shouted from his desk: "Ross." Mason got up, looked doubtfully at Lantho, who looked out of the window and said nothing, and then went into the inner office.

"Ross," said Mr Stewart, "Your examination result was pretty good, and I'm glad to welcome you as a member of staff here. I hope you'll stay with us a long time. The working hours are from eight thirty until five thirty, Saturdays eight thirty to twelve thirty, Sundays off, a week's holiday during the summer, all Bank Holidays. All matters concerning the bank and its customers are confidential and not to be talked about anywhere. You will not be expected to enter Public Houses in this village. You are expected to put a tenth of your salary into your own bank account each time you are paid. Your first pay comes at the end of your first fortnight, on Saturday week. Those are the rules, Ross, and I don't think you will find them too burdensome. Lantho and I keep them. Now the best thing for you to do is to work with Lantho and pick up the business from him, and if there is anything you do not understand then you may come to me and ask. I hope you will be happy here, Ross, and that you like the work and that you will remain Neat, Clean, and Efficient. Now you had better go out to the counter and help Lantho, because customers will be coming in now."

Ross went back to his desk. Lantho was still entering figures in a big ledger. "Open up the shop, Boy," he said.

"How?" said Mason, because the door would open already; Mr Stewart had walked through without unlocking it.

Lantho leaned forward from his place and gave the blind on the back of the door a tug. It rolled up immediately and the dangling string of it, with wooden knob on, danced in the newly-let-in light and tapped on the glass. Sunshine lit the words on the glass of the door and wrote "Vendale" on the floor.

"That's it, open," said Lantho. He went back to his writing. Mason went back to his.

"Boy," said Lantho, closing his ledger with a thud, "here's our first customer."

The word "Vendale" on the floor was blotted out by the shadow of a head. The belonging body walked in through the door and laid a cloth bag on the counter in front of Lantho. "Now it's a grand day again," said the owner of the head.

"It is," said Lantho, solemnly. "Boy, get Mr Fawcett's book out. Look sharp."

"New lad," said Mr Fawcett. "Ross, isn't it?"

"That's so," said Lantho. "Have you found it yet, Boy?"

"I don't know where to look," said Mason. "There's so many books and ledgers on those shelves, it's like a quarry; some of it's rock and some of it's rubbish, and there isn't a name to any of them, just numbers."

"Just like a quarry," said Lantho, "every bit numbered."

He got down from the stool he sat on and came to help. "I'll instruct you later," he said. "It's this one, number 43."

Mason put the big ledger on Lantho's desk. Lantho told him

66

to open it. Mason opened it. Inside the cover there was a red patterned shiny paper, and a printed label saying: "Edward Fawcett Esq., Bridge Inn." Mason turned on to the first empty page. Meanwhile Mr Fawcett undid his cloth bag and began laying out the contents.

The contents were money. Notes and silver and copper, thrown in unsorted. Mr Fawcett tired of lifting handfuls out and tipped half out when he was halfway down. "That lad will make a Banker," said Mr Fawcett. "He never takes his eyes off the brass."

"Staring, I dare say," said Lantho in a melancholy way. "Boy, look sharp and get this money counted. Mr Fawcett has to get back to his clients; he hasn't got all day, and nor have you."

Mason had indeed been staring. He had seen as much money as this quite often, when the wages clerk came up on Fridays and Saturdays to pay wages at the quarry. That money did not belong to the clerk, but to the directors of the quarry. And it was given to the quarrymen so that it was spread out into so many sums that they were no longer connected together. But this money, heaped on the wood by Mr Fawcett belonged to Mr Fawcett, all of it, and was being put into Mr Fawcett's account in the bank. And perhaps he brought as much each week.

"Count it, Boy," said Lantho. Mason began to count. Lantho began to make entries in the ledger.

Mason had not thought about counting money before. He took it coin by coin, moving each counted one from left to right. He reached twenty nine shillings and eightpence half-penny, then dropped three coins, picked them up, and went on with the count for some time before noticing that he was counting from right to left and was approaching two pounds and was lost.

"You're not framing," said Lantho. "Look." He began to flick coins with three or four fingers, off the edge of the table and into the other hand, and stacking neat castles of coin along the back of the desk, twelves of copper, eight of half-crowns, tens of florins, twenties of shillings and forties of sixpences. The little silver threepenny pieces, eighty to the pound, he put into paper bags without counting, and weighed, dropping in sixpenny pieces until the weight was right. He left Mason to count the notes. There were other papers too, not very familiar to Mason, with amounts written on them and signed. One of the papers was signed by Jedediah. When every coin and note and paper was reduced to order the amounts were totalled and entered in the book. Mr Fawcett inspected the book, folded up the empty bag, said "Good morning," and went out.

"Those are cheques," said Lantho, when Mason asked about the papers that were written, not printed. "Some of them are as good as printed bank notes, some aren't. That Spitalhouse one, for instance, that's been a good signature for a number of years; so have these here. There are some I don't know. But you can write a cheque for any money you have in the bank and pay it to anybody. It's an order to your bank to pay it out."

"What if you tell them to pay out more than you've got?" said Mason. "What then?"

"Trouble," said Lantho. "That's what's then, Boy."

They had other customers before half past twelve. When it was that time Lantho brought out a sandwich and some cold tea in a bottle, and had his meal. "Did you bring no bait?" he asked.

"I never thought," said Mason.

"You'd best be off home and get something," said Lantho. "Be sharp, again, Boy. We've to catch the train at quarter past."

"Train?" said Mason. "Where? Why?"

"You look sharp, I said," said Lantho. "Or there'll be no how or when or where or why or which or what or whom and whose or whence or whither."

Mason ran home up the lane, a quicker way than waiting for the next truck on the Incline. On the way he had time, though, to consider why his hands were so dirty and smelled so bitter. It was from touching money. He licked one palm and the money taste gloved his tongue with the same thin metal and he had to spit among the butterflies.

"We aren't wanting you," said Mam, when he walked into the house.

"I've to have my dinner quick," said Mason. "We're off on the train at quarter past. I should have taken my dinner with me."

"You should," said Mam. "But your Dad working on top of the job I never gave it a thought. You always came in from school, and I knew it would be different, but I never meant to starve you. Well, sit and eat, and where are you off on the train, may I ask?"

"I don't know," said Mason. "He never had time to tell me. They gave me a pen with a feather first, but it bent up and didn't work."

Dad came in and had his dinner too. There was no time to talk about anything. Mason had his hurry to catch the train, and Dad had his, trying to organise the work of the quarry so

69

that as many men as possible were able to work each day. Until the crane was mended there was one section that could not be worked because nothing else would lift the big slabs required. Dad was trying to work out which order they could deal with next, digging out different rocks in different layers of the quarry.

Lantho was not at the Bank when Mason got down there just after one o'clock. Mr Stewart was there, though, and told Mason to go on to the station and find Lantho waiting. Mason remembered that last time Lantho had had to be found down in the bottom of the town he had landed Mason in the river. Today he was peaceably on the station platform, and beside him were two large black boxes that Mason had seen in the Bank that morning, locked and in a corner.

"Where are we off?" said Mason.

"We have a shop in Dacre," said Lantho. "Mondays. Wednesdays in Birstwith and Fridays at Scarsgill."

The train came in, waited ten minutes with Mason and Lantho sitting in a compartment by themselves with the two black boxes, and then went out of that station and beside the river. They got out at the first stop, and carried the boxes out of the station.

There was no shop of the sort that Mason had expected. Lantho knocked at the door of a cottage a little way from the station. Outside the door of the cottage was a small plate with the name of the Bank on it, and "Monday, 2.00 p.m. to 3.30 p.m."

They were let into the cottage, and it was not like going into anyone's house. The housewife opened a door inside for them and showed them into a room and then went away.

"Shop," said Lantho. Mason thought it was a peculiar insistence to say it again when they were in a parlour. Lantho made it more shoplike by unlocking the boxes and setting them on a table. They both opened out into shelved cupboards and made a high counter. Mason sat and waited for something to happen. Lantho seemed just to sit and do nothing, not even wait. He was just there, looking at the wall.

They had nine customers. Lantho knew them all. None of them knew Mason, and Lantho called him his assistant. Mason counted money and noted the amounts in a book called "Cash Tally". He knew what that was because there was a Powder Tally at the quarry, so that it was quite clear how much explosive there was in the powder house.

Exactly at three thirty Lantho closed the boxes, told Mason to carry them out, and went to tell the housewife that they were going. Then they went into the station, where the same train was waiting for them, sat in the same compartment, and went backwards to the same place on the same platform that they had started from. Lantho yawned.

Mason thought that the day so far had not consisted of work. He carried the two boxes up from the station, with Lantho walking in front. That at least was work he understood. He did not see that he could have been useful in any other way, apart from a few lines of writing that Lantho might have done quicker. When they got back Lantho said that he would see about the boxes this time because a Boy would not know what to do. He could watch, however.

He was not to watch, however. Mr Stewart shouted, "Ross," and he went through.

Mr Stewart had a small packet for him to deliver in the town, to a place he knew quite well, Bishopside Hall, for Jedediah Spitalhouse.

"Don't get gossiping," said Mr Stewart. "I reckon you can be there and back in quarter of an hour," and he looked at his watch.

Mason went into the front room of the Bank and was just going out of the door when Lantho called him back and asked him where he thought he was going.

"Jed's," said Mason. "On a message."

"Mister Spitalhouse," said Lantho. "Everybody's mister that has to do with us, mister Ross."

"Yes, Mr Lantho," said Mason.

"What are you taking him?" said Lantho.

"I don't know," said Mason.

"I'll find out," said Lantho. "Get on then, Boy."

Mason got on, up the High Street, then along to the Church as if he were going home. He held the packet firmly. It might contain a hundred pounds, he thought. Then he felt that amount was too large and settled for seventy five, which was quite a lot too. But he had spent the day moving money about and writing it down and grown used to thinking in pounds instead of pennies.

He passed the lane end and a field later crossed the Incline on the road bridge. He came to the gate of Jedediah's house and walked in and up the drive.

He thought, all at once, and for the first time, that he might see Moira. Instantly he was listening and watching, but all he sensed was his own heart beating louder. He rang the front door bell. He supposed that was right. Jedediah's housekeeper, Mrs Maddock, came to the door and asked him what he wanted. He said it was a message from the Bank. Mrs Maddock was suitably impressed, he thought, because she asked him to step inside and wait while she went to find Mr Spitalhouse. He waited in a hall that he knew well, where he had always before been a visitor, not a messenger, where he had always come free, not being paid to do so.

Jedediah kept him waiting longer than five minutes. He felt the quarter of an hour going by and going by. Then he came.

"It's you lad, is it?" he said. "They took you on then."

"Today," said Mason.

"Right enough," said Jedediah. "Well, let's have your message and then you can be off. Is it hard work there?"

Mason handed him the packet, and he tore it open. "Nay," he said, "this is no good, lad, no good at all." Mason knew he was angry because there was creeping into his voice the tone that he had used on Dad two days before.

"It's what Mr Stewart gave me," said Mason.

"Of course it is," said Jedediah. "Don't be so fond, lad; I know you've brought what he gave you, but it won't do, I can't make it do, not any way. I'll have to write a note, and see whether he can do better. You wait here again; I'll not be a moment."

Mason waited. For company he had the wrapper of the packet, lying crumpled on a small side table. It was expanding gently as it lay there, and making a small rustling noise. Perhaps it was to flatten itself out entirely before Jedediah came back.

It stopped moving. Jedediah came back with a note in an envelope. He had smudged the ink of the name on the outside, The Manager, Vendale Bank. When he gave it to Mason he gave him a threepenny piece as well, warm and silver and un-weighably small by itself.

When he came back to the Bank Mr Stewart had gone.

"He'll speak to you in the morning," said Lantho. "You've been gone out of your time, he says."

"I had to wait on Jed. Mr Spitalhouse," said Mason. "He sent back this note." Lantho took the note and put it in his pocket.

"I can't open that," he said. "I'm not the manager."

"What shall I tell Mr Spitalhouse?" said Mason.

"Nothing," said Lantho. "Nothing, Boy. How could you? You don't know anything, do you?"

"No," said Mason. "I don't."

But when Lantho told him it was time to go he felt guilty about not going to Jedediah's again when he was obviously expected. He did not know whether he ought to go there and say that Mr Stewart had left for the night, or whether he ought to do nothing. He went home by the Incline, because that would give him time to think about and a moment on the way up by the gate when he could jump off the truck and take the message.

He came past the house and saw no one there. Then there was a shout towards him from the truck coming down, and Peter Ward called something to him, going twice as fast as the gate on the other side. The opportunity to give a message passed him between all the movements, and he went home for his tea.

VI

MASON CAME IN through the back door of the house, hungrily hoping that tea would be ready. It was not. Dad and Mam were sitting there talking to a policeman.

"Don't come in yet," said Mam. "We're just busy."

Mason wanted to know why. At first it was curiosity, why should the policeman be there and no tea ready. Then it was more than curiosity; to have tea delayed and nowhere near ready meant that something unusual was happening, and policemen mean that the unusual thing might be a bad one. Mason waited in the yard, wondering what anyone could be guilty of. He did not think he had guilt, or nothing very recent. Perhaps he had committed some crime at school, like carving his name where it should not be carved. He had often thought about cutting it into the outer door under the school tower, but he had never done it. He felt guilty about it, all the same.

He could see the policeman through the window. Dad and Mam were looking grave. The policeman was writing in his notebook. They sat, still, and Mason tired of being in the yard.

Feeling guilty about one thing, even if it had not happened, made him guilty about another, which hadn't happened either but in a different way. He ought, he knew, to have stopped at Bishopside Hall and told Jedediah what had happened to his note. He knew that Jedediah wanted a message

75

back from the Bank. Of course, the policeman had not come about that, but that became the thing he felt most guilty of. He walked back to the top of the Incline and looked down.

There were no wagons moving. The men had gone, and the last empty truck had been drawn up. The cable lay slack on its rollers at the top of the slope. The brakeman's hut beside the line was empty and locked. The quarry was silent. There was no noise even from the dock at the bottom of the Incline. It was all mysteriously calm, as if half a century had gone by and no work had recently been done. Then fifty years dropped away, and a horse drawing a wagon came out of one of the quarry cuttings and towards its stable.

Mason started down the Incline. He might, after all, see Moira, he thought, though it was not a thought that seemed to him important. He was really going to Bishopside Hall to hide from the thought of the policeman and the meanings his presence could have.

He came to the side door of the house and tapped on the glass of it. No one seemed to hear, even after the fourth time. He turned from that door and went round the end of the house, through the stables and the motor house yard. He passed the nursery windows, set low in the ground, and let his eye look in. The room was empty, no Moira was there; all the same, muscle in his chest moved and interrupted a breath he was breathing. She will come in, he thought, she *will*, and with the tremendous persuasion and need for her to appear he felt that she almost did, and that if he had only been able to think with more of himself, to use all the power of his will, she would have come from wherever she was and been in the room below, if not in reality then as a passing vision or mirage.

There was the front door. He rang the bell. Mrs Maddock came and raised her eyebrows at him. She left him in the hall again and sent for Jedediah.

"Good lad," said Jedediah. He felt in his pocket. Mason noticed how the deepest tones of Jedediah's voice echoed round the hall. Jedediah brought out a coin, and began to put it in Mason's hand. "You've brought it then, have you?" he said.

"No," said Mason. "Mr Stewart had gone home when I got back. I gave the letter to Lantho."

"Lantho, by God," said Jedediah. "You shouldn't have done that, but you aren't to know." The coin in Jedediah's hand, almost pressed into Mason's, withdrew itself. Jedediah's hand went back to his own pocket and stayed there. "Have you been home yet?" he asked.

"Aye," said Mason, meaning that he had and he hadn't and twisting the sound of the word so that its meaning changed.

"Have they settled owt yet?" said Jedediah. "I mean, has the investigation yielded any fruit?"

"I don't know," said Mason. "Did you send the bobby up there?"

"Never," said Jedediah. "But I saw him go up, and I know what it's about."

"I don't," said Mason. "What have they done?"

"They've lost forever of blasting powder and shots and stuff," said Jedediah. "They left some shots in over the week end and they've been taken, and when it comes to it the Powder Tally isn't anywhere near. So that's what the bobby's up there for, and that's what he's investigating."

"That's all right, then," said Mason. He could see that it was a serious matter, but not one to feel guilty about. Dad could hardly help it if somebody stole from the quarry, and could not be blamed.

"It's right enough so far," said Jedediah. "If that's as far as it goes. Thank you for bringing the message, Mason." Jedediah turned away from him and went into one of the rooms. Mason stood in the hall. Mrs Maddock came and showed him out of the front door.

He climbed the Incline. As he went up he saw the policeman going down the lane by himself.

At home tea was being got ready, quietly. Dad was sitting in his chair by the fire, thinking or brooding. Mam was doing her own brooding and being sympathetic at the same time. Mason came in and sat at the table.

"You can get your hands washed, quarryman," said Mam.

"They smell of money," said Mason.

"You get close to things, you smell of them," said Mam.

Mason washed his hands and came to the towel by the fire.

"How much powder did they take?" he asked.

"How do you know about it?" asked Dad. "Does everybody know?"

"Jed told me," said Mason. "He said the Tallies weren't right. We have Cash Tallies at the Bank."

"There's a fair bit gone," said Dad. "We don't know how long gone, that's the worst. Whoever took it covered up and hid the theft. But I get blamed for it. It's against the law to steal it, and it's against the law to lose it. But it's Jedediah and the other directors that get the blame for losing it. They get fined in court, and I just lose my job, and that costs me more than a fine costs them."

"You shouldn't have called the policeman up," said Mam.
"I had to," said Dad. "And now we'll see what happens."

*   *   *

Mason's days had changed from what they used to be. School used to begin at nine o'clock and end at half past three. Now his days began at half past eight and ended at half past five. The first days of this length were new to him, and passed quickly. But the second week was not such an exploration; he had no need to keep his wits about him so closely, and during the long hot afternoons of the middle of July he more than once found himself propped against his desk in a breathlessly unconscious mood that was really sleep. The breathlessness was caused by the collar and its way of biting into his neck if he let his head fall to one side.

"You get used to it," said Lantho. "You get used to life, you get used to being what you are, and it has to go on, or nearly all of it does. Boy."

"Yes Sir," said Mason, and bent back to his column of figures that he still added one by one. Lantho added by looking and tightening his lips and moving his tongue in his mouth. Dad did his adding by looking at the figures and writing down a figure that he thought might be a reasonable answer. He did it by 'geg o't'ee', gauging by eye, and then pecked at it later until it came right. The amounts of stone, which is what he calculated, were always right, because his geg o't'ee was perfect on real things like wagons and quoins and cills and lintels, flags and piers and slates. Adding them up when they were not there was difficult for him. Mason wondered whether that was why the Powder Tally had gone wrong, and whether the

79

amount of powder was right and only the addition was out of truth.

The end of the school term came. One day there was no sign of children in the streets when he came by, and the school gate was locked. Mason felt then that he had been looking forward to his holiday, but had become caught in the next part of the world.

Even the matter of money earned made no difference. Before he got it the Bank took some back and laid it in an account for him. Lantho told him he was never to draw it out, and that one day he would be glad of it. Mason wanted to be glad of it now. When he got home with his first money Mam took it all from him and gave him back the pocket money she sometimes had for him. The rest, she said, was not enough for him to live on, and it didn't make up for what he cost her to keep in food and clothes now, never mind all the years before he had earned anything. Mason did not know what to do about it. Most of all he had looked forward to having money that was his own, and to have it taken away before he had the feel of it was a disappointment that took the edge from his pleasure.

Peter Ward was no better off, though. His mother took all his money too, and there was not even some hidden in the Bank. They had between them a few copper coins, and that was all.

"No good trailing off to the Nanny Goat Inn," said Peter. "Waste of a walk, that would be." Mason agreed with him, and was pleased that he did not have to decide whether to be scorned by the world for not getting sick on ale, or shamed by Mam for doing so. Now there was no choice to be made.

He saw Moira one evening, coming from the train with Jedediah and Fräulein. Fräulein was carrying the coats,

Jedediah was carrying a rug and a small case. Moira was carrying, with both hands, a basket of strawberries.

"We've sold our motor car," she said. "It was more trouble than it was worth, wasn't it, Daddy."

"A sight too much bother," said Jedediah. "It wasn't a very good make, happen."

Moira giggled when he said "Happen". "Strawberries," she said, changing the subject. "Don't they look lovely? They're the first ones." She did not offer him one.

"Come on, you both," said Jedediah. "Moira, Fräulein."

So they went to the bottom of the Incline and up it in a truck. Mason thought about strawberries crushed in his mouth, and remembered wild raspberries in the wood at the end of the quarry, and thought that Moira was to him like strawberries tasted with the heart, not the tongue, like the rock flavour of the universe that he had understood when he looked at the bones of the rabbit under the green raspberries.

One night, as they tidied the Bank before leaving it, Lantho gave him a piece of paper with a mark on it. He had just made the mark with his pen. "You don't have to walk home," he said. "With that."

Mason could understand nothing of that. It was as if all his memory had failed, and that he should have known, or as if there were more worlds than he had known about and this was something out of one of them. He had to say he did not know what it was.

"It's done with a pen," said Lantho. He did not smile or seem interested. "It is an ink-line. You just ride on one of the trucks and you'll be home."

"Yes," said Mason, still not understanding. Lantho closed

the Bank door behind them and they went different ways. Mason studied his paper, and gradually saw the relationship between an ink line and an incline, and that Lantho had given him a joke. He took it home in his turn and showed it to Mam. She said that Lantho was a queer one, and she could not make it into a joke, just into something that made her uneasy.

She was uneasy in any case, and not patient with new things. Dad was more than uneasy; he was worried. His worry was very apparent to Mam, but Mason had to be told that his father was worrying. Otherwise he seemed only out of temper, and his left arm hurt, or what was more remarkable, the hand hurt that he no longer had, and when lost fingers ache there is nothing that can be done. Sometimes they ached and sometimes they felt hot, which was worse.

The quarry was not working well. The ten-ton crane was not to be repaired in a hurry. A part had been ordered for it but had not come. Jedediah had been up and complained that there should have been a spare, but there was none. Jedediah had blamed Dad again, and the men blamed him as well. Dad was brave enough to go out and tell them that there was no work, and therefore no money, but being brave did not stop him from dreading the task. The men would come in the morning and as the days passed the number who could remain grew less and less. In the third week after the crane broke only one gang was wanted, and the rest stopped coming.

"And at that," said Dad, "there's not full work for them all, but it has to be a gang or none."

The crane was not the only trouble. A bad sample of coal came up and choked the boiler in the saw-sheds, so the saws stopped working, the fires had to go out and the flues be cleaned.

Dad was blamed by the directors for not sending on the coal bills after checking them for weight and quality, so that the directors had not been able to pay the coal factor, which was why he had sent inferior coal.

Then Mason, riding up the Incline one evening, heard the talk in a descending truck, as it approached and passed him, the voices coming clearer and clearer above the mutter of the wheels on the rails. The voices said, distinctly, that Tommy Ross had been up to mischief, or things would not be as they were now, and who was to blame if suppliers went without their money but the man who should have paid them, Tommy Ross.

Mason knew it was not true, that the way the quarry was run did not allow his father to handle money; all the bills were paid by the directors, and all Dad did with them was say whether the goods had been supplied. But the slowly moving men in the other truck said more. There wasn't any doubt, they said, that coal, and waste iron rails, and blasting powder, hay for the horses, certain loads of stone, had all been got rid of quietly by Tommy Ross. The rumbling of the truck wheels drowned the rest of what was said. Mason wished he had heard none of it. He looked after the retreating wagon, and one face looked back at him: Peter Ward. Peter Ward was the useful boy in the gang, and though he was the newest taken on, the gang he was in happened to be the one still working. Peter lifted one hand a little and then did not wave it. Mason did not wave at all, but looked the other way.

There was Moira, with Fräulein, standing in the grounds of Bishopside Hall. She waved. Mason took no notice, and thought she would have to understand that he did not want any notice taken of him until he had taken in what he had heard and looked at it and then somehow rejected it. What harm could come to her, he thought, secure as she was in all the fortune of a wealthy father, with no prospect of want, with no man to master her parent, with no shadows of imagined deceit hanging over her, with a solid house they owned, with all that she could want. And she had not offered him a strawberry. He thought then that he hated and resented the fascination that she had for him, that he would fight all the impulses that led him to glorify her, that made her something like light in the ordinary shadow of living. He tried to think away from her, but none of him would let her go except part of his mind. It was for her remoteness and difference that he loved her and hated her, and the two ways of regarding her kept her more firmly at the centre of his attention when he saw her or suddenly came upon her among his thoughts.

Why should he hate her as well? he wondered. That was a new sense for him to explore. It was not understandable, but it was there. Then, just as he found himself growing hot and red with frustrated anger, his hate melted away, and, too late for the day, he turned to wave to her. But she had gone, and he himself was trapped in the rising wagon unable to get out. The wagon took him over the top of the Incline and among the sidings, and stopped. He got out, full of many thoughts, of what he had heard from the other rail, of what he had experienced on seeing Moira from the threatened base he stood on if what the man said was true. When he got home all the mental sensations were washed away by the physical one of a good hot meal waiting.

On another day he saw her pass the Bank, not with Fräulein

but with the Irishwoman, her mother. This time he was immersed in his work in a way that surprised him each time he found himself at it. He was able to do two things at once: to carry on adding up slowly but steadily, and to think about Moira at the same time. The thoughts were not very clear and not about a person but more about being part of a world that contained someone who mattered as much as Moira did.

"Wake up, Boy," said Lantho. "I'm going to talk to Mr Stewart. Keep the shop."

Mason had kept the shop before and dealt with customers on his own. This time he was wishing that Moira would come in and ask for money when the door opened and she came in. After her came the Irishwoman.

Mason stood up. Lantho usually stood up for lady customers, except when he was in the little cottages of the branch banks.

"Mason Ross, is it?" said the Irishwoman. "You look for all the world like a real official, presiding there; are you printing banknotes?"

"He's in business here, Mummy," said Moira. "Aren't you?"

"Yes," said Mason. "It's like work, only it's business."

Mr Stewart put his head round the door. He nodded to Mrs Spitalhouse, and said: "Carry on, Ross. I think you can manage." Then he went in again.

"If Mr Stewart thinks you can do it you'll be as good as him," said Mrs Spitalhouse. "It's not me to serve but Moira. She knows what she's about, don't you darling?"

Moira had two pounds and three shillings to put into her account. Mason had a little trouble at first finding the right book because he did not know what kind of account it was.

Then he located it, took the money in, and entered it in its columns.

"There you are, madam," he said, just as Lantho did.

"He's very apt at it," said the Irishwoman.

"Why didn't you wave at me the other night?" said Moira, pulling on a white glove.

"Because you had all those strawberries and didn't give me one the time before when I saw you," said Mason.

"You couldn't eat it in the street," said Moira. "If you wanted one why didn't you come to the house?" She and her mother started to leave the Bank. "He's a silly boy sometimes," said Moira, clearly to all the world. "He never comes to see me and he really loves me, he said so." Then the door closed after them and the next words were mere mouthings beyond the glass. Mason snapped the ledger shut, banged it on the shelf, and felt betrayed by Moira's words to her mother. He felt confused too by the realisation that she knew he loved her and yet did not understand it either.

Lantho came out of the inner office, got down the ledger that Mason had dealt with, examined the entry in silence, checked the cash tally, and went to his own place. Mason said nothing. Lantho had once loved the Irishwoman, and probably still did, Mason judged, since he could not see that anyone could ever stop loving once they had started. So it would not be right to let Lantho know that his love had been heard of. Love is too private a matter to be told, even to the one you love, Mason thought: to have told Moira was to have given his thoughts to anybody, because Moira did not understand. In a way, perhaps, he had not shown any of his feelings; they were still his. For Lantho it might have been worse, and the Irishwoman could have understood and still rejected his love. After all, Jedediah had married her in the end. And now neither of them had her.

"Bait time," said Lantho, leaning over and pulling down the blind to discourage customers while they ate their sandwiches.

VII

THE REGULAR SEVEN O'CLOCK blasting stopped punctuating the day. Mason still woke up at seven but his mother had stopped the automatic duty of opening the windows. Now she had warning if there was to be a blast. The quarry was short of other noises too; sawing stopped early and started late; horses stood idle; wagons were not moved. The days that began silently felt like Sundays or holidays. To go down to breakfast in a Sunday suit seemed natural, but then to go down to the Bank with the weekday activity of the village round him seemed strange.

There was less village activity as well, though there were more people about in the street. The number of men working had fallen to about a quarter of its usual level, and only a quarter of the usual amount of money was being spent. The shops opened later. This year the only strawberries Mason saw were the ones Moira had carried through the street; the shops did not buy any. Two girls who had left school at the same time as Mason, and begun work in shops, Lizzy Holmes at Pickersgill's the drapers, and Ruth Scaife in Wharton's grocery shop, lost their jobs. Mason had not seen them since leaving school, but now he began to see them each day, both as he went to the Bank and as they passed the windows during the day. Lizzy Holmes would wave at him as she went by sometimes.

Other things changed too. Small blue butterflies flew in the fields. The honeysuckle heaped on the wall of the lane at one place sat in a pool of its own flowers and sweet sweaty smell. Mason remembered from an earlier year, long past, when he and Moira had searched the withies of its growth for the elfin engines they thought must be there, operating saws and cranes, not seeing what made the noise until Mam told them: the insects drunk with the scent.

Lantho and Mr Stewart spent long times conferring together, and Mr Stewart went to talk with Jedediah. Lantho went away for two days once, and came back full of important matters that did not come to Mason's ears. He had the key of the Bank for one night, and had to let himself in one morning, timing his opening by the church clock. Then he entered his own office and moved quietly in its silence, more like a visitor than an entitled person.

"Anything fresh?" asked Mr Stewart when he came in.

There was nothing fresh. Mason had picked up the letters and put them on Mr Stewart's desk and then gone on with the usual and daily work of keeping all the accounts up to date.

"Good boy," said Mr Stewart. Lantho was back the next morning, and Mason handed over the key and let him open the door. Lantho picked up the letters and gave one piece of mail to Mason. It was addressed to him, and he looked at it with surprise. It was a postcard from Leeds, with a picture on one side, and the address and the message on the other. The picture was of two holiday-making gentlemen on the sea-front beside a bulging tent. The bulges of the tent were caused by the arms, legs, and body of a stout lady in the tent. She was pulling on a pair of very frilly drawers. One holiday-making gentleman was saying to the other: "I wonder what's going on in there!"

The message said "Wish you were here," and was not signed.

"Remarkable," said Lantho, when he saw it, without a smile. "Who could have sent that? Some lady-friend?"

Mason hoped not. That is, he hoped it was not sent by Moira, but he could have understood if it had been sent by Lizzy Holmes. He put the card in his desk. Lantho went to confer with Mr Stewart.

Two days later Mr Stewart called Mason into the room and asked him to sit down. "We have to have a talk," he said. "Now, tell me, how do you like the banking business?"

"It's all right," said Mason.

"Which bits do you like best?" said Mr Stewart.

"I like writing it up neat," said Mason. "And I'm getting to like the adding up, but I can't do it like Lantho yet."

"Lantho is brilliant but unsound," said Mr Stewart. "Now and then he makes a big mistake and doesn't check his work. So far you haven't made many mistakes, apart from adding in the date once or twice."

Mason felt himself redden. "Did I?" he asked. Mr Stewart handed over a sheet of paper. Mason saw that a date had been written under the pounds, shillings, and pence, and added in. "I didn't write that," he said, because he knew, without being able to say why, that it was not his work, though it seemed to be his writing.

Mr Stewart took the paper back. "One of Lantho's jokes," he said. "We get used to those. So you didn't make that mistake. You've done well, Mason. What else do you like?"

"Going to the branch banks," said Mason. "I like the train

90

ride, and they give us cups of tea now they know we won't tell you."

"I did know," said Mr Stewart. "Just wait a minute, Ross." He went out into the other office and closed the door. He came back a few minutes later and said: "That's given him something to think about. But now, lad, I want you to listen carefully. You'll have seen how trade is at present. You know better than anyone how the work is up at the quarry, and you'll know how many families depend on it. You know that there isn't the work there now. The other places of business in the town have got rid of new staff; the place is full of folk with nothing to do. Now I'll be quite plain about it: the Bank ought to dismiss you, because there isn't the work for you, and we're paying money for nothing. There's hardly the work for me and Lantho, but it still takes two to run this office and the branches. We are both taking a cut in our salaries, but you shouldn't tell anyone that. What I've got to say to you is that we either dismiss you, or you go on working for pocket money, just your savings and a few shillings, until times get better. No, don't say anything now; go home and ask your parents what they think."

"I know what they think," said Mason, "without asking them. If I didn't do any work they'd still have to feed me, so they wouldn't care that way, but they would like me to work, and I would like to work."

"Money doesn't mean much to you," said Mr Stewart.

"I don't get it anyway," said Mason.

"We'll leave it like that," said Mr Stewart. "You'll go on working for pocket-money for the time being. But if things get much worse even that will have to stop. And things may get

91

a lot worse yet, Ross; believe me, I know more about it than anyone. I think I may be out of business myself before too many weeks are past."

Lantho was in the outer office, about to eat his sandwiches. He did not speak. Sometimes he would talk over his dinner. Today was Scarsgill branch day, and after his dinner Lantho would usually check the boxes and fill up the float, the loose change and cash that went to the branches. Today he did nothing about it, but went on writing in the ledgers.

"Scarsgill," said Mason. "Today, Lantho."

"Not me," said Lantho. "You heard him. Accusing me of taking beverages at Birstwith, drinks at Dacre and swipes at Scarsgill. Came and told me he was running a Bank not a Bar. So if I'm not trusted then you'll have to go alone. You know how to do it."

"It was his joke," said Mason.

"Ha," said Lantho. "I'll help you with the boxes to the station."

Mason went alone to Scarsgill, transacted the day's business, and came back. There was nothing about the day that he could not deal with. The only thing he felt slightly guilty about was coming home with less money than he had taken, because people were drawing money out rather than putting it in. But that was the same in all the Bank business now, and it seemed strange that business could exist like that, though Lantho had often said that it didn't matter which way the money was moving, the Bank kept a little of it, it stuck to their fingers. Mason smelt the bronze money on his own fingers: the smell was being part of him now.

His mother was not surprised by his news. Any work was

better than no work at all, she said, and it could all turn out well in the end.

The next day was Saturday. It was normally a busy morning at the Bank, with wives bringing in small savings from the previous day's wage packets. Now there were no wages to save from, and few wives came in, because they managed on what they had from the Parish Relief, and did not want to break into savings until they had to. There was not much to do but look from the window at a rainy morning. Mason saw his mother come by and give him a smile. She went on up the street and into the grocer's shop. But she got no further than the doorway, where there was the big wife of a laid-off quarryman, who was angry at not being able to spend what she thought was necessary for her family. Mam came up behind her, and the woman turned on her and started to rave and rant. They all knew, she said, what the trouble was up at the quarry. They knew who'd laid hands on the money that should have been used for keeping the machines running. They all knew who had the ear of Jedediah Spitalhouse and who twisted him round to think as he did, there wasn't a better man than Jedediah and none of this trouble was his fault, it was just the people who told him lies, those who'd got him in their power. They all knew who wasn't out of work; they all knew where Jedediah's favours were, and nobody was going to mind how well-off Jedediah was, they knew that he did his best for his workers and he had a hard enough time bringing up that little lass without being advised to his ruin, and he lived off the quarry as well as the rest of the village, and while wealth did not bring happiness, neither did poverty.

Mrs Ross had stepped back out of the shop doorway, and

waited for an opportunity to say something mild and reasonable. Other women came up to calm the quarryman's wife, but instead of soothing her they caught her rage. Like Mam they waited for a break in her speech, at first for an opening to say quieting words, but when the time came they first had to say something vicious to Mam and then it was too late for what they had intended. Mam became surrounded by other women, and then, somehow, the women were arguing among themselves and Mam was coming down the street alone. Mason went out to meet her, and found her walking with tears on her face.

"It's not true," she said. "They're wrong. It's all Jedediah's fault, not ours, but I can't tell them, I can't tell them." She would not stop walking, and Mason walked with her in the rain, down to the bottom of the street and then along to the Incline. There was no truck moving on it, so they walked up it, alongside the abandoned rope, beside the cut hay-fields lying damp and flat under the moving rain.

"We won't tell your Dad," said Mam, when they came to the top of the Incline. "There's no need."

"He'll know there's summat," said Mason. "Your nose is red."

"And you're without your coat," said Mam. "It's a vexing time, and that's all there is to it."

"And I came out without my money," said Mason. "I came out before the end of the day."

"You shouldn't," said Mam. "No, you shouldn't. I should have sent you back, but I'm glad you came out, Mason. I don't know how I could have walked alone out through those streets. She isn't a wicked woman, that Elsie, but she has more to put up with than she ought to have."

They met Peter Ward, coming wet out of the saw-sheds. "Now then," said Mason, much more cheerily than he meant.

"Oh, aye," said Peter, walking by and then stopping. "Have you got laid off yet, Mason?"

"Just about," said Mason. "Have you?"

"No," said Peter. "But they take all my brass at home, so there's no ale at the Nanny Goat for me, and I doubt they'd not let you in. Is it true about your Dad taking all that money?"

"No," said Mason. "Don't you start on with that," and he gave Peter a blow on the side of the head, more in anger than in remonstrative friendship.

"It's only a bloody question," said Peter, and then with new quarryman muscles that he had none of the last time Mason fought him at school, he knocked Mason down among the stones and chippings and wet dust, and left him there.

*   *   *

"Half money, is that it, Jedediah?" said Dad.

"That's it, Tommy," said Jedediah. It was Sunday morning, and still a wet day. Jedediah had come at about nine o'clock and been looking into papers in the office for two hours.

"I don't like it," said Dad.

"It's my living as well as yours," said Jedediah. "I'm doing without a good deal more than half just now."

"Your all was bigger than my all," said Dad. "And I'm doing the same amount of work as I was."

"You've only a quarter of the men on now," said Jedediah.

"It doesn't matter how many men," said Dad, "there's all the back work to it, all to oversee. It's more work with the one gang than with all four. But I know I'm lucky not to be in a laid-off gang."

"I heard they were getting nasty," said Jedediah.

"More than that," said Dad. He had during the night had the whole story of the grocer's doorway from Mam. "There's a story going about that I don't like, Jedediah Spitalhouse."

"You haven't given me my full name like that in thirty years." said Jedediah. "Not since we were little fighting lads in that school yard down there."

"I'm not bothered about that," said Dad. "I hear of a nasty tale all the old women are having a call about, and that's what I'm talking about."

"It's not my tale," said Jedediah. "I'm not telling it, Tommy."

"But you've not got up and faced them and denied it," said Dad. "Have you, Jedediah?"

"No," said Jedediah. "I'm not taking sides, Tommy, that's what. I don't know the truth of it, do I?"

"Of course you do," said Dad.

"No," said Jedediah. "It doesn't matter what I believe, Tommy. It all has to balance by the books, and the directors are looking at the books now, and when they've looked they'll tell me, and I'll know. But I don't know until then, Tommy. If I thought it was true you wouldn't be here now, lad. You can see I'm trusting you, but in the end it's the shareholders that have to be told, and the only thing that'll tell them is the books. So I can say nowt, Tommy. But it's half pay, and that's better for you than for a lot of folk."

*   *   *

Mam spent a lot of Sunday struggling with Mason's suit, wet with rain as it was, and stained deep with stone dust. It was ready to wear on Monday, smelling scorched from being pressed with hot irons. The Monday collar bit his neck.

He was early at the Bank door, and waited there for Lantho.

"I kept your money," said Lantho. "I said I'd sent you on an errand, so he doesn't know."

"Good," said Mason. But when Mr Stewart came in he stopped by Mason's desk and said: "I was sorry to hear about your great grandmother's funeral on Saturday, Ross. I hope you got there in time."

Lantho was behind a joke somewhere, Mason could see, but he could do nothing about it except say that his great grandmother was very well, thank you Sir.

"Enjoyed her funeral, eh?" said Mr Stewart.

"Yes Sir," said Mason. "She'd been looking forward to it . . ." and he heard what he had been saying. "Oh Sir, it's him again," he said.

Mr Stewart went into his office.

On Tuesday Jedediah sent word up to the quarry that half the horses were to be hired out to farmers for the hay harvest, because there was not work for them and they were eating money. It had happened before, Dad said, but not during his time of managing, or even during the time he had worked in the quarry. He had a feeling that it was the worst sign so far, and that the next would be the selling of the horses.

There was a sign on Wednesday as well. The manager of another quarry in the next dale came and bought one of the smaller seven ton cranes, and on Thursday sent a gang of men to dismantle it and carry it away in horse-drawn carts. Dad stood by and would have nothing to do with it, apart from writing to Jedediah and protesting that no one had sent him a single piece of paper about it, and that he wasn't going to be responsible for losing a crane. The smith was on his side about the affair, and signed his name, Bucko Robinson, at the foot of the letter, saying that Jedediah had sold the crane, not Tommy Ross.

On Tuesday evening Lantho had another joke. "Which way are you going home?" he asked Mason.

Mason said he was going the usual way, up on an empty truck that was pulled up by the last full one down, if he didn't have to stop too long talking to Lantho.

"If you do stop too long," said Lantho, "I'll buy you a lazy dog. An idle cur."

"Why?" said Mason.

"It's a slow pup," said Lantho. "A slope up. And a slope up is an incline."

"Yes," said Mason. "But you've had that joke once, only with different words."

"That's how jokes are," said Lantho. "Different words all the time. Like poems, they keep ending with the same sounds in different words, only there it's rhymes, not laughing."

As he went along to the foot of the Incline Mason whistled for the imaginary dog. But it was indeed a slow pup and never caught him.

VIII

THE SAWING-SHED CHIMNEY did not smoke at the week end: the fire was out again. There came from the stack of stone a sour smell of cold soot, borne on a chill breeze that fell from low grey cloud. The day was dark on Sunday, and the stone that stood everywhere in the quarry was damp in the morning and dried slowly. Mam said it was ironing-damp, when she laid her hand on the edge of the single stone that was the scullery roof.

Dad was having to clean the flue of the sawing-shed steam engine, because the bad coal had thickened on it and lessened the steam. Mam said she was not going to church, because nobody had spoken to her there for weeks, and she didn't go there to be ignored by anyone, no matter who it was. She built up the fire, sent Mason across to the sawing sheds to sort out some half-burnt coals from the contents of the engine, and did some baking.

It was a pie for dinner today, instead of a piece of meat. Mason thought pie was an improvement on roast beef or mutton, but Mam thought it was a cheap substitute, which was why she made the pie.

"A week or two with the best amount coming into the house we ever had," she said, with the knife singing round the pie-dish cutting off a ribbon of surplus pastry. "We had your

Dad's money, and we had yours, and the bonus for the extra stone that week. And now, half pay, and nothing from you, and you've never eaten more in your life, and you've never grown so fast since you were a year old and then you cost nothing to feed. You and that lass of Jedediah's I was feeding one time. That Irishwoman could never manage any of a mother's duty."

The knife stabbed the crust of the pie. Mam cut leaves from the spare scraps and laid them damped on the top. The pie waited until it was time for it to go into the oven. Dad came into the house through the back door. He brought with him a stronger smell of soot and cold clinker than the breeze had carried. He began to wash noisily, splashing water on the floor, dipping his head in the bowl and spitting and sniffing to get rid of soot in his head. He came through dripping with his hand scratched raw by the work he had done, and where it was scratched raw it was bedded black. He began to rub himself with the towel.

"That's a grand pie," he said. "A good figure of a pie is that. And a good figure of a pie-maker," and he put his dried left arm round Mam and hugged her with it.

"Give up," she said. "There'll be the buns burnt in the oven if you don't leave loose, Tommy Ross. And take your wet hair out of my face and stop mauling me." She stamped on his foot. Dad dried his hair and brushed it down, rolled down his sleeves, buttoned up the left one and put his arm out for Mason to button the right one, and sat by the fire.

Mason, sitting by the table and reading, found that he was happy. He was hungry and would soon be fed; he was warm, he was at home; he had a place in the world; he thought it was certain that Moira would one day love him, because he loved her, and if you loved someone surely the rule was that they began to love you; if the rule was not so why should you ever love at all?

Mam began to clear the cooking things from the table and to lay it with eating things. Mason thought he must be right. For hunger there was provided food, so for loving there must be returned love, the only match. He found he was thinking of ideas, not of people. He thought about Moira, trying to bring those eyes to the visionary part of his mind, with the hope that the thought, like love itself, would bring the actuality, the matching thing, into being. But instead of Moira his mind brought him a sharp picture of Lizzy Holmes, unexpected, unwanted, and unactual.

"Wake up," said Mam. "Dreaming there, get your book off the table, Mason."

"Oh, me," said Mason. "I'm hungry." Food was his most need now, and his mind stopped wandering and concentrated on his plate.

After dinner there was a time when he could not think what to do for the rest of the day, or the rest of his life. He began to despair of ever knowing when he saw that Dad solved the same difficulty by going to sleep in front of the fire, like a cat. Mason saw him stretch the fingers of either hand, the right one luxuriously so that the fingers whitened, and the left one with a similar movement but ending in a ghost: all the muscles still left worked, and Dad probably felt the fingers move. Then he slept, relaxed.

Mason was in most of the same mood, but not relaxed. He got up, took a long drink of water, and went outdoors. Mam had had her nap by the fire, and got up at the same time. She went upstairs to get things to mend and make the beds.

Mason flung stones in the quarry for a time, then stalked a rabbit that had come out from its burrow in one of the older tips. The rabbit became annoyed, stamped its foot, and went to shelter. Mason looked round for another rabbit. He saw something bobbing about beyond the wall of a field above the quarry face, and went up to see what it was, over the slipped slope where the top had not been taken away to bare rock yet. He came out on the heather-covered slope of the bank retaining the small reservoir for the water the machinery used. Beyond the grey water in its square of bank was a track, and along the track walked Fräulein and skipped Moira, accompanying her.

Moira, in a teasing circuit round Fräulein, turned and saw Mason. She stood and waved like a windmill, meaning that he had to keep quiet. He kept quiet, because he would do anything she wanted, and caught up with her. She pulled him round behind the end of a broken wall, and said "Hush, let her get all lost," and they both watched her through the gaps in the wall.

Mason reckoned that Fräulein had seen them and was not going to bother to call Moira to order.

"She's quite happy," said Moira. "She didn't want me to come with her but there isn't anybody else in the house, so I had to go. I think she goes to the Nanny Goat Inn when she can."

"Not on Saturday nights with the quarrymen," said Mason.

"No, only in the daytime," said Moira. "She likes the goat's milk, but she can't go if I'm with her because I can't go there."

"I don't think I can either," said Mason. "But I'm supposed to go with Peter Ward one day when we've got our money and have some ale."

Fräulein turned round now and shouted: "Mason, you shall take her home, please."

Mason stood up, now that he was directly addressed. Fräulein said "Yes?" and Mason said "Yes." Fräulein turned and strode away.

"She can go," said Mason, "like a good 'un."

"I can go faster," said Moira. Mason wished that Moira would leave Fräulein to go instead of bothering with her. He wanted the choice to be clear, that she was with him. He knew she loved Fräulein more than she loved him, but she might have changed; he wanted to see that she had changed. But for the time being they had to scout along behind the wall, until the wall turned away from Fräulein and it was impossible to say they were following any more. They sat on the wall and watched her approach the Nanny Goat Inn, half a mile away along the hill.

"We'll go home now," said Moira. "Are we near the quarry horses? You can show me them. Where do they live?"

Mason said they would go past the stables. But first Moira had to throw stones into the reservoir for quite a long time, wondering why the surface of the water mended itself so well each time, smoothing out from a jagged edge to a living, dying, ripple, squaring against the edge. Mason studied a centipede, moving slowly across a rock like a mobile scar ready to be scratched.

Moira examined it. She said she had a better scar at home to show him, but she hadn't it with her now. Then they went to the horses in their stable. The stables were empty of all but the smell of horse. Half the horses were working for farmers, and the others were grazing quietly in a field. They went to look, but the creatures did not wish to be caught or touched, only to eat, and they walked away from Moira at her most coaxing, knowing perhaps that she had nothing in her stretched-out hand for them.

"My horse has gone," she said. "My horse has gone, we sold him to a little girl down the dale. I'm going to have a bigger one before long, as soon as Daddy sees the right one. I'm growing up, you see, and when you grow up you don't want a horse older than you. That one was getting older than me."

"It was always older than you," said Mason. "It was older than me."

"Horse years are different," said Moira. "Mason, what is there the other side of the Nanny Goat Inn?"

"They keep the ale at the back," said Mason.

"I mean the places," said Moira. "What places are there? What happens at the top of the hill? Is it different up there?"

"Moorland," said Mason. "Rabbits and that."

"Fräulein doesn't know," said Moira. "That's how I know she doesn't go any further. Now take me home." She climbed over the gate of the horses' field, and put out a hand for him to help her down. He helped her, and then wanted to go on holding the hand. But Moira only wanted to run down the hill, and he had to run with her. They ran to the lane and then it was single file down among the rocks. The butterflies, blue or brown, moved slowly. The tall spikes of the foxglove hung overhead, heavily beaded with green below the climbing steeple of flowers that were purple, and yellow above where they were still scales. Heavy bees went in and out of the doors in these steeples.

"I love you," said Mason, loving her and the lane and the flowers and even the heavy day.

"That's what all the boys say," said Moira. "Do you like butter?" She had pulled a buttercup and thrust it under Mason's chin. "Yes, you do."

"What boys?" said Mason. There were no other boys that he knew of. "When?"

"I expect they'll say it," said Moira. "I've got a rich Daddy, so they're bound to say it, aren't they? Mummy says they will."

"I'm not them," said Mason.

"It's tea time," said Moira. "I'm sure it is. We have to go home."

"But if there isn't anybody there there won't be any tea," said Mason.

"There will be," said Moira. "There always is, and if there isn't we can get some from somewhere."

"And I still love you," said Mason.

"I like you," said Moira. "But I don't expect I'll love anybody until I'm quite old."

"Older than a horse," said Mason.

"Much older," said Moira. "And now let's hold hands and run all down the lane."

Bishopside Hall was empty, overhung with the green trees, caverned. Moira led him in through the side door, and then was daunted by the silence. No one heard, no one came; no voice or footfall but her own echoed in the entries and stair-well.

"Fräulein," she shouted.

"She can't be here by now," said Mason.

"She can be in two places at once," said Moira. "If she's been on goat's milk again. Goats are different." But she was not here. Moira shouted for Hilda, "though I know she's gone home." There was still silent unresponding air. "Maddock," she shouted, at last, but not with such a loud voice. "That's the proper way to call housekeepers," she said, grown a little pink with temerity, "but I usually call her Mrs Maddock, and anyway she isn't here either."

"We could go outside again," said Mason. He felt that neither of them had any right in the house alone; even Moira ought not to be here without some special permission.

"No," said Moira. "I'll hide, and you can seek. You go by the clock and count fifty." She ran away, waving to him to hide his eyes. He did so reluctantly, and counted up to fifty. It was not his house, and he was not properly invited, and, suddenly, he was alone. She was not in sight and she was not within his knowledge, and he had to look for her, an immodest proceeding. He found her easily the first time, and then expected her to seek him, but she would do nothing of the sort: he had to seek again, setting a compulsory silence between them, unless he wanted to count aloud.

He found her in the drawing room, kneeling by the piano. "Do you play?" she said. "Listen." She bent attentively over the keyboard and touched it with her fingertips, bringing a tune from it, dark hair bonneting her face, blacker than its own shadow. She stopped on a wrong note, and corrected it. "Mason," she said, angling a second time for the right note and losing it again. "Well, it ends like that. Mason, What's your Dad done?"

"Nothing," said Mason. "Of course he hasn't."

"Daddy knows he has," said Moira. "I heard him."

"No," said Mason. "How could he?" But he knew that he could not explain that he was sure Dad had not done anything amiss at the quarry, that everything was bad luck and not fault. He could not explain to himself, and he knew it would be difficult to explain to Moira and bring her to understand even if he did know.

"I don't know how," said Moira. "But it's something dreadful, isn't it?" She looked at him to see whether dreadfulness was exhibiting itself in him; she was excited by the idea, and wanted to know dreadful people, if they were no different from themselves as she knew them.

They were standing next to the piano now, by a table with great legs and a shining top. On the top, reflected and double-reflected, and glittering among themselves and deep in the wood, were sharply decorated glass bottles with coloured liquids in them. Round their necks were silver labels. Moira picked one off, ran a finger over the word on it, Brandy, and slipped it on her wrist. "It's Daddy's quarry," she said.

An empty bottle said Claret. Mason took off its label and put it on Moira's other wrist. They took all the labels now, Whisky, Gin, Rum, Port, Sherry, Cointreau, and hung them on her wrists. Then, when she had rattled them and felt the weight of them she thought they should put them back. They did not know where each one should go. Moira thought Mason should be able to tell by the smell, but to him, when he smelt one bottle and another, they smelt of camphor, like Fräulein. Moira giggled at the thought, and then they stood without moving, because there was a noise in the lobby by the front door, and someone walked in.

107

"Her," said Moira. "I hope she didn't hear."

Mason took the handful of labels and draped them on the bottles in any order, and followed Moira out to the hall.

It was the Irishwoman who had come in. "Mummy," said Moira. "And I don't believe there's anyone in to make the tea."

"Sure, isn't that how I like it?" said Mrs Spitalhouse. "Is it true, no one in at all but you and a young man?"

"No one," said Moira. "I shouted."

"Then we'll be into the kitchen and get ourselves some tea," said Mrs Spitalhouse. "Isn't that how I like it to be and it never is?"

"I've got to be off now," said Mason. He was no longer part of what went on, no longer sharing anything in this house, not part of Moira and the Irishwoman.

"What have you done to be ashamed of?" said Mrs Spital-house. "And we're not proud. Come into the kitchen."

They went into the kitchen, a part of the house that Mason understood better than the rest, because home was kitchen, a middle room that had to be walked through, and a scullery with a sink and one stone slab for a roof.

"This is fun," said Moira, bringing plates and cups from the dresser to the table. "The kettle right on the fire."

"That's the place for it," said the Irishwoman. "The kettle should be on the fire, or where's a tinker's trade?"

"M . . . Mrs Maddock uses the gas," said Moira.

"Gas and motor cars will blow your head off one day," said Mrs Spitalhouse. "Money doesn't master your fate. Moira, be off and find a jug of milk and some sugar, and a knife to cut some breads. Mason, you rattle that fire into life."

Mason rattled the fire, and the kettle began to croon to itself. Moira was in the larder beyond somewhere, looking for milk now, and the butter, and what cakes there were.

"Tell me," said the Irishwoman, "is it bad days up at the quarry?"

"Yes," said Mason. "There isn't much left up there to work on, and Jedediah's blaming my Dad and he's having to do all the work like rattling the fire up there for the saws."

"While you rattle the fires down here for us," said the Irishwoman. "And both Jedediah's fires. He has too many fires, that's the truth, Mason. I should have kept him in better order, but I haven't a long enough temper. I wonder, is it worth trying still."

"Are you coming back, then?" said Mason.

"Never to this house," said the Irishwoman. "Now there's a red fire you have, be toasting these breads I've cut and keep the coal-reek off them."

They had tea, sitting round the fire and at the table, with toast in the hearth, the teapot up against the fire, the cake on a chair where it would be 'better mastered', said Mrs Spitalhouse. Towards the end of the meal another person came in. Fräulein had returned. She came into the kitchen, and was scandalised at the party going on there.

"It is not *höflich*," she said, "entertain in the kitchen, Moira, I am sorry Mrs Speetelhaus, *nicht war*."

"The only wicked part," said the Irishwoman, "is that we've bread and cake and butter and tea enough for twenty here, and just three of us to enjoy it, when there's many below in the town wondering whether today's bite wouldn't be better kept for tomorrow while you still have the choice of it."

109

"Madam," said Fräulein, blankly, because she was not going to listen or respond.

"Will you not have a cup of tea?" said the Irishwoman.

"It is time that Moira shall be in her bedroom," said Fräulein.

"Rubbish on you," said the Irishwoman. "I'm waving the teapot at you in welcome."

"Tso," said Fräulein, and she walked loftily out.

There was silence in the kitchen for a moment. Fräulein walked up the stairs.

"Mummy," said Moira. "Now I'll have to go to her. You don't know what you do. You're never just in the right place."

"No," said the Irishwoman. "I'm somehow always the wrong way on to the cart. Then run off if you have to, darling. I'll find my own way out."

Mason got up from the table, or fireside. He thought there was too much entanglement here, and no way of knowing which side would be Moira's side when all was clear. "Mam will be looking for me," he said.

"I've to show you something," said Moira. "Wait on and I'll get it. I mean, wait, and I'll get it. 'Wait on' is common talk." She ran out of the room and along to the nursery, and then upstairs.

"I'm no more use to her," said the Irishwoman. "I'm no use to anyone, except perhaps Jedediah, if I can bring him back to being a simple man like the one I married without this finery. But listen, Mason, will you not take a basket of things to your mother, there's plenty here and more than they can miss. Look, here's a basket, and I'll fill it; there's plenty I owe your mother."

"No," said Mason. "No, that's not right, Irishwoman."

"That's all I am?" she said.

"Nay, it's what they call you," said Mason. "But you can do nothing for my Mam that she would want, and what's here isn't yours, except Moira is, and you don't do anything for her, and you can't love her like a mother the way you are, coming and going, and I know my Mam isn't anything special in mothers, but she does love me and stay with us, and why don't you love Moira when you should and, and, and I can love her and I don't have to."

"Mason, Mason," she said. "It's more than that, Mason. You see how I am: what can I give her that she can't be given better for what she has to be?"

Moira came running back into the room. She was carrying Loosan.

"There now, see," she said. "What did Fräulein say? Lungs and livers and things. She has put them all back. Look." She lifted up Loosan's dress, and below it there was the cloth body, restuffed, re-sewn with a white thread.

"Like a scar," said Moira. "See, feather stitch, so neat and small. And look." She gave him a blushing look and lifted Loosan's dress higher. Above the white stitched scar, on the heart side, and on the other side too, of the cloth chest, was stitched a little pink bosomy silk knot. Mason saw, and then the dress was pulled down. "Fancy, Fräulein," said Moira. "Kiss Loosan goodnight, Mason."

Loosan approached his face twice, banging him on either cheek, and was then dropped on the table. Moira ran out of the room again and up the stairs, calling to Fräulein.

"She's to grow older yet," said the Irishwoman. "A year or two."

"Horse years are different," said Mason. But he was wondering whether he had fallen in love with Loosan or Moira, or which was which.

"It's donkeys' years in the end," said the Irishwoman. "Donkeys' years."

IX

THE MIDDLE ROOM at home had become inverted. The lamp was not in the middle of the ceiling throwing light and shadow down and making an overhead white. It was on the floor and throwing whiteness up from the spread of paper that Dad studied on his knees.

"Step between them, Mason," he said. "But it's between them I want to be myself, because what I want isn't here. Jedediah has had first look at these, and there's papers I know I've seen that I can't find, and he must have taken them. Well, go on, lad, don't leave the door open."

Mason stepped through the drift of paper and went into the kitchen.

"There's your tea waiting," said Mam.

"Sorry," said Mason.

"It's no matter," said Mam. "I can't get cleared till he's done with that lot in there. It's not the first time he's had them out, wasting oil in broad daylight, but he can't see down on the floor on a dull day like this. He won't find it anyway, the directors have fixed that."

"He said," said Mason. "I don't think I need any tea, I've had some."

"You needn't say where you've been," said Mam. "I know. I saw you going past the stable, and she's been moulting on you again," and she pulled from his sleeve two or three long dark hairs. "I doubt it never gets a good brushing these days. Still, you've to go with who you like, Mason, but why it has to be that one, now, I can't tell."

"Maybe I will have just a piece of pie," said Mason, sitting at the table. Mam automatically poured him a cup of tea.

"You'd think I'd brewed cinders," she said, looking at the rusty liquid.

Next door Dad swore to himself. "He gets bothered," said Mam. "He puts out his hand to move the lamp and he can't. One night he'll knock it over and there won't be any papers at all."

"Perhaps that would be better," said Mason.

"Happen," said Mam. "But nothing will make any difference now. Jed has to have it his way, as usual, and if he says 'Go' it'll be go, and no more work for us. Dad just wants to show he did his best, but he can't find much to go on."

Mason ate his pie, drank his tea, and had some bread and butter. He needed a little more filling after the untidy meal at Bishopside Hall. Dad gathered up his papers, banged them into their boxes, and came through with the lamp. Double light flooded the kitchen. Mam got up and turned the wick down and seemed to put out the sun.

"I'm off out," said Dad. "I can make neither sense nor meaning of that lot." He went out of the house. "You stop in," he said to Mason, as he pulled the door shut behind him.

"Say nowt," said Mam to Mason. "He means don't be going down to Jed's every minute."

"I don't," said Mason. "And I don't see Jedediah if I do."

"They're all of a flock, he thinks," said Mam.

114

And Mason wondered. There was the Irishwoman, who was not part of anything, and Fräulein who just worked there, and they were both something apart from the flock, if there was one. The doll with the embroidered chest was not part of any world Dad could fear. Mason himself was carried by it because it was outspokenly indelicate, and while it could not be private to Loosan because she was only an insentient doll, it was private to Moira and Fräulein. He had been startled by the embroidery. But before that, before the kitchen tea he had been made uneasy by Moira's reference to some bad thing Dad must have done. Was it possible that Dad had not been the good steward of Jedediah's quarry, that what Moira suggested might be true? It was a cloudy suggestion, and that made it no better. Moira could know better than almost anyone what was in Jedediah's mind.

"We'll get washed up," said Mam. "Come out of your dream, Mason," and she gave him a cheering thump to wake him.

*   *   *

On Monday, after he and Lantho had eaten their sandwiches and were getting the box ready to go to Dacre for the banking afternoon there, he saw Moira go past with Fräulein. He watched for a moment, but they were in different worlds: there was more than the glass of the door between them; there was all the routine of business that he could not break through, and for her there was all the business of being herself. Mason suddenly wondered how she found room to regard him at all.

"Enter that float in the Cash Tally," said Lantho. "You know how it's done."

Mason knew how it was done, and he knew what the words meant, which was part of his new knowledge. But he had let his mind wander to Moira, and forgotten part of the business routine. He found that there was more to seeing her than being glad of her presence. Now he had something to ask her, something to find out from her.

They took the boxes down to the train. Mason found they were following Moira, who went ahead of them on to the platform, and to the front of the train and got into one of the remote and expensive First Class compartments. Mason wondered whether they had luxurious cushioned tickets with lace edges. Loosan's drawers had lace edges. Moira had not seen him and was not in sight. Mason looked out of the window the far side and saw the river and wagonloads of stone waiting to be moved along. The engine moved past and Lantho reached across and put the window up to keep out the swirl of smoke and steam.

They got out at Dacre without seeing Moira. She was not on the return train either. Mason had waited for her to be, ready to go to her, whether it was the Bank's time or not, and ask her what she knew about Dad. His expectation was wasted for the time being, but his resolve was not abated. It was possible that she had come back by some other means while he was at Dacre, or in the Bank afterwards. Instead of waiting for a truck to ride home on he walked from the foot of the Incline up beside the track. From the dock at the bottom the Incline seemed today like a cut or wound laid across the fields, inscribed on some of them, below their level, and on others laid like a stick over the curves, almost separated from the ground below.

The house beside the Incline was quiet. There was no sign of any occupation. Mason went to the front door and pulled at the bell, waiting until someone came at last. It was Mrs Maddock. There was no one in, she said. She did not know any future arrangements of any member of the house, except herself, and she was leaving later that evening. "For another appointment," she said.

Mason said "Thank you, Madam," in a suitably Lantho-ish manner, and went back to the Incline and up it and home.

He watched the approaches to Bishopside Hall from the top of the hill after tea. To get there from the village Moira would have to come along the road or up the Incline, and both ways were visible. He watched for a long time, and then Mam called him to sift cinders for the fire. So he did not see her, and when the cinder-sifting was done it was too late in the day to set off anywhere.

The morning was still and misty underfoot. The lane was hung with drops of water, and the hay-fields between it and the Incline were full of it, rising and hiding the hard edges of the ground. The blasting was late these days, and came when Mason was among the rocks. There was the faintest quaver through the ground, accompanying and following the noise, and there was a fast fall of drops of dew and mist from the flowers and extremities of branches. They seemed to spit and then stand taller.

The village was below the mist-line. Mason came through its smoke, lying along the hill, and into another clearness where the ground was dry. Sunshine came after him and sat in the Bank with him and Lantho. Outside the bank Lizzy Holmes stood, and ran, and teased, idle and unoccupied. She was teasing both Mason and Lantho. At first she leaned on the window, tapping it with one finger, able to stand high enough to see over the painted section and look, like something appearing out of the mud of an aquarium, out of the captivity of the street into the unbreathable airs of the bank.

"Don't look in that direction," said Lantho. "Work on; they'll go away."

Mason worked on. Lizzy squeaked at the window with her fingers. Lantho put out an arm and rattled on the glass as he had rattled at Mason a few weeks before, on that first day. Lizzy went away. Mr Stewart came. Lantho ran up the blind on the door. Lizzy flung the door open, shouted "Shop," and ran away at once.

"It's never the right lady," said Lantho, getting up and closing the door.

"Showing off," said Mason. Then he thought it was interesting that he was really showing off just as much as Lizzy, but he had proper work to show off with. He was glad to have Lizzy to show off to: Moira was not the sort that noticed what anyone else did, but Lizzy obviously had noticed, and wanted to distract him, and perhaps Lantho too.

Customers came. They were taking money out, not putting it in. Mason had to go across to one of the other banks and collect some cash for their funds.

There was a long slack time during the morning when nothing happened. They had counted the new money; no customers walked in; Lizzy Holmes had gone away. Lantho tipped his stool back and looked at the ceiling. Mason yawned. Lantho yawned. Mr Stewart was very silent in his office.

Jedediah walked by. Lantho turned his head slowly to watch. Mason put down the pen he had been biting and wondered whether to run out after Jedediah and ask him, himself, what Dad had done. But it was Banking Hours. Lantho began to look in ledgers, as if he were checking and confirming something he already knew. "Jedediah," he said "I wonder what you are up to. We all wonder what you are up to, don't we, Mason?"

"Yes," said Mason. "We all wonder."

"I wonder what's going on in there," said Lantho. "Send us a postcard about it, Mr Spitalhouse. Now it's bait time, Mason."

"I've to go a message first," said Mason. Now he was sure that Moira at least would be at home, and Jedediah might be as well, or he might have been going for a train, or anywhere but home.

"Right," said Lantho. "Take your time."

Mason went out and up the street. Lizzy Holmes ran in front of him and then walked behind him kicking his heels. He hated her for doing it, and for existing, and for not being Moira. She did not leave the High Street.

Fräulein came to the door when he rang. The door had been open, and he had heard her voice and Moira's calling each other from room to room, with some note of alarm in their intonations.

"You are being too early, it is not *fertig*, not ready," said Fräulein, beginning to speak to him before she came in sight of him. Then she said: "Moira, it is only a friend, for you please. Well, Mason, it is perhaps conwenient; I do not know."

Then she dabbed her eyes, which were red, and instead of handing Mason on to Moira she put her arms round him and gave him a large hug. She smelt of the Sunday camphory smell. "You are perhaps unfortunate only," she said. "Und not yourselve wicked so much, Mason?"

"I don't know," said Mason, but he was a little dizzy from coming up to the house fast with no dinner, and then having the last short breath pushed out of him by the hug and having to take in a lungful of Fräulein's scent.

Moira came down the stairs then, carrying a straw hat-box. He saw that there was other luggage stacked in the hall.

"Are you off somewhere?" he said. "Is it holidays?" He remembered that the Spitalhouse family went to Bridlington in the summer, and wished he had had more time to think about it before seeing Moira vanish.

"No," said Moira, in a high-up strange voice he had not heard before. "Not holidays. Fräulein's going away. Daddy says she has to go home today."

"It is very *plötzlich;* it is also sudden," said Fräulein. "And I have done nothings *verkehrt*, what is it, wrong?"

"Maddock went yesterday," said Moira. "And Daddy came back last night and told Fräulein."

Their voices were now beginning to accuse Mason, as if he had dismissed Mrs Maddock yesterday, Fräulein today, and would proceed to more perverse acts tomorrow. "What next, then?" he said, to show that since he did not possibly know he was not the instigator of these deeds. Then he realised what might be next, if Jedediah was casting people out. Mrs Maddock was not the first. Before her had gone the car and its driver, and the pony Moira rode and whoever looked after it, presumably. And next there could be the Ross family: Dad as overseer of the quarry, and Mason as an almost unpaid banker;

both gifts were Jedediah's to withhold if he pleased, neither of them being gifts given for ever.

"There is a train coming for me soon," said Fräulein. "I have a home ticket been given." She hurried upstairs again.

"Have you been laid off too?" said Moira. "Is everybody going to be? It can't just be your Dad, can it? He isn't really one of the people Daddy talks about."

"I came to ask you," said Mason. "I mean, I'm still at the Bank, but they're given over paying me, but what did you say about my Dad on Sunday? because you never finished."

"Oh, nothing," said Moira. "I don't know. I didn't see anything. Now I've got to help Fräulein with her hat, and you can't come upstairs, you're a boy now."

"I'll wait," said Mason. Moira ran upstairs after Fräulein, and out of sight along a carpeted corridor. He heard her and Fräulein exchange greetings, and a door bang. He concluded that they were locked together now in some room discussing hats or gloves or camphor. He stood, and might have been in an empty house. He thought he might turn and walk out and leave.

A door the far side of the hall opened, and Moira stood in the shadows beyond it. It was Jedediah's study, and she had come to it by the back stairs. She looked at him, and went again. Mason thought she meant him to stay, and he stood where he was, full of intensity about nothing; the present was buzzingly important but important in vain. He watched the next events: the coming of a car from the station to call for the luggage, the coming down of Fräulein from upstairs, with the hat pinned firmly on and Moira mournful but excited by the occasion following and at last reluctant to show any affection in her farewell because so many people, one of them Fräulein herself, watched.

Fräulein's last words were: "When I am gone you shall eat your lunch, Moira. You see she shall, Mason." Then with a kiss and a clasping of hands she had gone and the camphor was replaced by the dry smoke of the station car.

Moira walked obediently into the dining room and sat before the small bowls, plates and numerous silver of her lunch. There was a lordly smell of pickles from the sideboard. Mason's stomach rattled in him; he felt as if he, like Loosan, had been opened at the heart and emptied of sawdust. Moira dropped her knife and made him turn quickly to her, startled. His skin crept back, from having tightened. He felt the embroidered scar across him, and the two pink knots under his waistcoat pockets.

"I don't want anything," said Moira. She pushed the plate away from her. It was brisket on it, like marble, and Mason longed for it. Then Moira pushed the whole setting across the table. A spoon slid across on to the floor, and a glass of water rolled and spilled and fell, water cascading off the table into the broken fragments and darkening the carpet.

Mason knew now that he was being unfair, that to ask what he had come to ask was untimely, that Moira had now had her life broken in a way he could only shallowly understand. He knew she loved Fräulein perhaps most of the people she knew; he knew that he was somehow bound to be in the consequences of the unknown act that had begun the disruption and that Moira was a fellow-sufferer. But he had to ask what she meant, what she knew, what she had nearly said.

"What did Jedediah say about my Dad?" he asked. "If you know you have to tell me, because he didn't do it."

Moira left the room. Mason followed. She led him into the study, where she had stood before in the shadows. There was a big roll-topped desk open against one wall, and papers were on it. It was not those that Moira indicated. She pulled open a drawer and inside it there was a printed paper.

At the top of the paper was the name of the quarry company and a picture of the workings. Mason saw his own house. Lower down there was a heading in black type: REPORT OF THE DIRECTORS TO BE LAID BEFORE THE SHAREHOLDERS AT AN EXTRAORDINARY GENERAL MEETING, to be held in Leeds on Wednesday of the next week. Mason had seen such papers before: they came into the house every year, sometimes a good many copies, and before the year was out they were used as spills or for making lists and drawings. They were usually for an Ordinary, not an Extra-ordinary meeting. At the bottom was Jedediah Spitalhouse, printed large, and called Chairman.

"Read it," said Moira. "You'll know about your Dad."

Mason read, with his eyes skipping from line to line until he bent his head down and steadied it with his hand. There were a great many figures, and some mechanical details. There was a paragraph that said: "During recent months it has become apparent that a deficiency in the manner of overseeing has led to severe damage in some of the machinery. At first it was assumed that negligence had caused the breakdown of the large crane and the injury of a workman, but it gradually became clear to your directors that over some years the overseer, Mr Thomas Ross, has not merely been forgetful of his duties, but has successfully hidden from discovery the fact that monies entrusted to him for reparations and maintenance have not been used for such purposes and are no longer in the

123

company accounts. Your directors cannot escape the conclusion that Mr Ross is a dishonest servant and that the monies have been stolen by him. Enquiries are at the moment proceeding, but it is necessary to reveal that such are the depredations on this account that it is extremely unlikely that any profit will be made in the current trading year unless the money can be recovered."

Mason picked the paper up. He heard his breath coming in and out of his mouth. Moira was standing close to him, reading the paper with him. "You," he said, "how could you know about it?"

"I hate you," said Moira. "I hate you. I hope he gets hanged for it."

"Moira, Moira," said Mason. "It can't be like that."

"It says it," said Moira. "Give it back."

"It's only Jedediah saying it," said Mason. "And I won't give it back."

"Yes," said Moira. "He knows. Give it back." But Mason was not going to give the paper back. Moira snatched at it, and he pulled her away by her hair, and then hit her in the face as if she had been any fighting boy at school. Then she scratched him with her nails across the cheek, and he ran out of the house, and she went upstairs wailing. He did not know what to do now: on the one hand was the paper, and on the other was Moira, and his heart was truly torn between two activities, so that he walked up and down on the gravel outside the front door of the house, unable to go in again, unable to turn towards home and display the paper.

A shuddering calm came upon him. He found his nose needed blowing, and that blood and tears stood on his cheek. But his duty was plain. He walked down the drive, along the road, down the High Street, and into the Bank, and sat at his place, looking at the ledgers in front of him.

"What the devil have you been doing?" said Lantho. " Half an hour late. There's been dozens of customers asking for you."

X

"No one waited for me," said Mason.

"No," said Lantho. "But I thought it would brighten you up. You look as if they'd suddenly put thirteen pence to a shilling and your sums won't total."

"I can't tell," said Mason. Certainly no figures on the pages in front of him meant anything now. Instead of the neat columns graved there by Lantho or Mr Stewart, and somewhat given a shake where his own hand took over, he saw Jedediah's cold print about dishonest servants and stolen monies.

"You haven't had your bait," said Lantho. There was the little cloth packet that held his dinner, still stacked with small books on one of the shelves. Mason turned his head and looked at it. Instead of it he saw the banquet place of Moira's meal, untouched, then scattered, and the glass and the water that ran and ebbed through the carpet. He knew how Moira could not eat, because her world was spinning no more and there was nothing to hold her to it and no way of living for it; and his own world had been checked the same way, losing its gravity and pull and, because of its unfamiliar feel, seeming to reject him.

"Don't fancy it," he said.

"Eaten too many gooseberries," said Lantho. "Is that it?"

"I had some gooseberry pie yesterday," said Mason. "But I don't feel bad, just not hungry."

"Been in the bushes," said Lantho. "To get scratched like that, must have been."

Mason put his hand to his cheek and felt his blood dried there.

"You want to get out the back and tidied up," said Lantho. "Get on; they'll think there's been a bank robbery if you're like that."

Mason went out to the Bank lavatory at the back of the building, where there was a tiny mirror and a tap in the wall. He looked at himself green in the light filtered through an elder tree. He damped his handkerchief at the tap and dabbed his face. He set it bleeding again and had to wait until it stopped before returning to his desk.

"Where have you been?" said Lantho. He leaned over and pulled down the blind on the glass door. "There won't be any customers," he said. "There's no money to put in, and there's precious little to take out. So what have you been doing?"

"I haven't done anything," said Mason. He knew he had done nothing that concerned the world beyond Jedediah and the quarry. Lantho was not part of that world, Lantho was not tied in the middle of its honesties and lovings. And Lantho had not done the final deed by which Mason had put himself in peril of Jedediah's, and Moira's wrath: Lantho had not struck Moira, or pulled her hair.

"Come off it," said Lantho. "Where did you go? Halfway up the Incline?"

"Part way," said Mason, not liking to admit fully that he had been to Bishopside Hall.

"You've been meddling, and got what you deserved," said Lantho. "But you aren't the first and the last, so you can go on with your work. There isn't anybody cares but you."

"Nobody cares," said Mason. "They won't keep me in the Bank."

"You don't know what they'll do," said Lantho. "You've kept your figures right. You've been civil to him in there, more than I have."

"I hit her," said Mason.

"That's different," said Lantho. "That's wrong, lad. That's violent. You can get into trouble for violence; it isn't a thing you want to start. How did you manage to hit her?"

"She hoped my Dad would get hanged," said Mason.

"What's he done?" said Lantho, "besides getting his arse kicked by anyone who wants to kick something."

"It's what Jedediah says he's done," said Mason. "She showed me this," and he brought out the report, smoothed it as flat as he could, and handed it to Lantho.

Lantho read it. Mason expected nothing but calm from him, and there was no strong reaction. He noted down the figures given in the report, and handed the paper back.

"It's powerful stuff," he said. "Things look bad, Mason."

"I know," said Mason. "They might put him in prison."

"They want to get on with it then," said Lantho. "If it's what Spitalhouse says then they should have had him up in court a bit since. No, things look worse for Jedediah, is what I mean. Jedediah's the one that's worried; the Spitalhouse empire isn't what it was, one way and another. And he's never got that house sold, either."

"House?" said Mason. "His own house?"

"Bishopside Hall," said Lantho. "It's been offered this last six weeks, and nobody wants to see it, let alone buy it and live in it. Well, who would, halfway between the quarry and the dock and those wagons down and up all the time."

"Selling it?" said Mason. "What for?"

"Money," said Lantho. "What do you think?" He took his new list of figures and began to compare them with what was written in some of his ledgers and files. "You wait," he said. "I know just how it is with Master Spitalhouse."

Mason looked at his own work again. It began to make sense to him once more. His hand against his cheek felt the slight scabs forming. His stomach sent up a message about Food Tallies and how things were not adding up down there. Mason wondered whether he would fold like Loosan, and felt a wave of affection for Moira break and plash inside him, and knew that he loved her again, and that it was a luxury. He put his hand out to the shelves and brought down the sandwiches. Lantho nodded to him, approving, and almost smiled.

An hour later the afternoon was like any other Tuesday. Mason spent the time preparing the books for audit at the end of the month. Lantho studied books that interested him more than they interested the bank. Mr Stewart sent Mason to the Post Office for stamps and to post the letters. The first time he went Lizzy Holmes was running up and down in the archway next to the Crown Inn, with a younger girl. She waved to him and shouted, but he did not hear on purpose. The second time she and the other girl were cornering a rat with sticks and stones behind some boxes in the archway. The rat was bored and not frightened and kept attempting to escape, and having to go back into temporary shelter, sauntering there without haste, contemptuous of Lizzy's skill with stick or stone, perhaps seeing that every time she hit at him she closed her eyes.

Lantho went early, after a private word with Mr Stewart.

"Have you cheered up?" he asked Mason before he went. "What you want is that lazy young dog again."

"The slow pup, the Incline?" said Mason.

"That's it," said Lantho. "Only this time it's a happy, lazy, young dog."

"Yes," said Mason. "Why?"

"Something to ride up in," said Lantho. Mason considered it, and found no meaning in it. He said so.

"Slow pup," said Lantho. "Happy slow pup: one end has a wag on. A wagon. To ride up on."

"I get it," said Mason. "It doesn't rhyme, like, but it fits the tune."

Those were the last words he was to speak to Lantho.

When he went out of the Bank at the end of the day Lizzy Holmes was swinging the dead rat by its tail, showing it as the trophy of her toil, exposing its clamping teeth at its lower jaw and the pale broad belly, as pleased with it as if it held money she would shortly tear out. Mason saw her hand on the animal, and knew how they were tainted with rat, even as far as resembling the curled dead claws, lithe-wake still. The smaller girl waited her turn to swing, and shared the glory.

Mason went home by the lane, not wanting to go close to Bishopside Hall. There was nothing for him there, he thought; how should she be able to speak to him again, or he with her? And now that he had the report in his hand, and was to show it at home, how could there be any relationship between the two houses?

He passed up the lane, and it was dead to him; there was not even in it the limpness of afterdeath as there was in the rat: all the limbs of his vision were stiffened, straining towards the further state of corrupt life when the horrors of the future would be inhabitants of the time that was to be. Dad would not be hanged, he knew: that was Moira's girlish anger, childish exclamation; but he might be disgraced, imprisoned, removed, a sort of burial.

"Tea will be a bit yet," said Mam, when he walked in. "Dad's at that steam engine, raking and scraping."

"I'll go and see," said Mason. His dinner had been late, and to wait for tea was nothing. He would in one way have liked tea to be ready now, so that he could sweep, like Moira, the table-load of pots and food to the ground. But he thought of the difference, the bright silver and glass and china plates, and the humble teapot and thick plates of home, and the rusting knives and green spoons and forks. The two gestures could not be the same.

"Waiting, are you?" said Dad. He was in the engine room beyond the sawing shed, raking and cleaning with the firebox still glowing and full of coals. "Best not come in, you'll be choked. I've just to rake among these tubes, or there'll be no steam tomorrow."

Dad could speak between clatters of the iron bars he was wielding, because he knew when he would rattle. Mason had to wait before he could speak. He looked into the fire, and caught the hot whiff of the invisible fume breaking back from the fire doors. The boiler itself rumbled and the feeder tank above it dripped. The hot day outside the engine room was dried at the doorway into something without temperature, and the radiance from the machine struck through dry and clean, not overpowering.

They both came out dazzled from the fire, stumbling on the clinker scattered at the threshold.

"Makes you sweat, that," said Dad. "But a healthy sweat."

"I got this," said Mason. There was no other way of saying it. He gave the report into Dad's dirty hand. He held it and read it where he stood, bringing up the lost left hand as if to hold the other edge of the sheet. When he had finished he let go with his right hand, but not, he thought, with the left. The paper floated away. Mason went to pick it up. Dad bent and picked up a great lump of browny blue clinker, held it for a moment, said a word that Mason did not catch, and threw the clinker out of the sawing shed, over the benches of stone, over the railway lines and the empty trucks, and through the window of his own bedroom.

"You," he said to Mason, calmly, "you get your teas. I'm off to see Jedediah. He'll not print that and hear nothing. I'll be back and have this sorted." He looked towards his left hand, whose fingers he must have let close on the paper, and found it and the paper missing. Mason gave it to him, and he went off across the railway lines, towards the top of the Incline.

"We've to get our tea," he said, flatly, when he went into the house again. "He's off to see Jedediah."

"Oh, he never said," said Mam.

"Jed says he's dishonest," said Mason. "He printed it. I got it off Moira and now I don't think she'll speak to me again."

"Who printed what?" said Mam. "I'll be off and see Jed myself, and that'll knock his print crooked, they'll never read it again."

Mason sat down and told Mam what he could. She was interested in the paper, and in Moira too, and by the end of what he told her she was furious with both of them, angry with the world, and was not quite on Mason's side either. Mason was left to be on his own side by himself, the same person he had always been, with the same feelings and sensations he had always known. It seemed to him that if you know about something then it happens before its occasion, before its time. When you and it get to the event there is nothing left to happen, nothing else to see. The shadow is before the thing.

Mam made the tea and drank four cups. Mason ate his tea. There was nothing else to do. Before he had finished, but late enough in the meal for him not be put off very much, Dad came back.

"He's not in yet, says the little lass," he said. "But he'll know when he is in: I'll be in with him and sort him out."

Mam looked at the paper. Mason saw her decide that there was nothing she could do but wait for what was to come. Her face tautened and became remote, like the face she had on her when she went to nurse the injured man. This time, though, she had only a mental bundle of used sheets for her equipment.

Dad ate his tea standing up. He went down to Bishopside Hall again when he had finished, and then twice more during the evening. Jedediah was not there.

"I'll sleep on it," he said. "Or maybe give him one more turn." At the beginning of darkness he went down once more. Mason watched him down the Incline, going into the dusk of the cutting and the shaping light of the banked section. There was no full darkness tonight except where mist touched the ground. Overhead the sky was steamy, not clear, but not cloudy.

Only four or five stars shone through a vapour that hung overhead.

Mason watched. There were lights in the village. There was noise. A motor car moved somewhere in the valley. At the joining of sky and land on every side there was a line, sometimes smooth, sometimes jagged, where the two elements touched. Though the tone of both was the same there was a distinctness about the meeting place, pencil mark on pencil.

A stone tumbled in the quarry. The boiler in the sawing sheds belched and sighed, livingly. On the Incline a pale mark bobbed. Dad came back, unsatisfied still.

"Just the Irishwoman," he said. "No sense out of her. She'll not stop the night, but she says she'll leave a message for Jedediah. But it won't be half the message I'd leave him if he was there to hear it."

XI

DAD WENT OUT to damp down the fire of the saw engine. It had been too big before he cleaned its flues and tubes, and was still too hot. If he had let it go out and then cleaned it another day's work would have been lost. Mason went with him for a time and watched the mouth of the fire open in the dark when Dad looked in.

"We'll get some of the steam off it," said Dad. "I'll not sleep tonight with that pain in my arm again." He lit a lamp and hung it smoking on the wall and began to lay out and adjust a slab of stone for trimming. "I can't see with this," he said. "My eyes are jumpy too. Get a lamp from the house, I can't frame with this smoking wick."

Mason went into the house and got the lamp from the middle room, and took it out with its rays into the night. Here new light shone from below, but upwards the light crept away, vanishing from sight and use. In the bigger area of the quarry it was possible to see the limits of the lamp's power. Mason walked in a flat circle of light to the building. It was possible, he thought, with the closely particled air of the night, and the waifs of steam hanging about, to see that he walked in a half-sphere, not just in the light on the ground but taking his dome with him. Perhaps the light completely fled outwards, visible only from some moon. He put the lamp on a stone table formed by a random grouping of slabs. By its light Dad adjusted the slab to be worked, cranking the saw-table with the hand cranks and laying the long blade of the saw over the marks to cut the bevel required.

Mam came out then and wanted to know two things. One was, who had thrown a great lump of something through the window upstairs, and when, and what was it, horses don't fly, do they?

Mason said it wasn't that, and Dad had thrown it. But he went up himself to get by candlelight the lump of clinker and threw it among the rails outside. Mam said she would clear the glass in the morning, or she would cut herself, and talking of cutting herself, Mason, how did he come to have a scratched face?

"Moira," said Mason. It was just a name to him now, with no more meaning than any other name. "When I got that paper."

"You'll have no right to the paper," said Mam. "But Jedediah has no right to have a paper saying that. What's your Dad doing?"

"Going to saw all night," said Mason. "He won't sleep."

"No, he won't," said Mam. "And nor will I with that thing rattling outside the window."

The saw itself breathed softly. Water ran under the blade and dripped out of the growing groove in the stone, saying a small beady sound with each drop. The steam sighed in a gentle breathing, slower than the saw. What rattled and chattered and clicked was the array of rods and gears between the fly-wheel and the saw. The best Dad could do with them was oil them.

Then, in the fine warm night he sat by the lamp and read the piece of paper again.

Mam put the kitchen light down low. Mason stood on a rail between the two lamps. For him now there was no firm place to be. He felt, or knew with certainty, that the house he had lived in was darkened for the last time, that its protective, light-reflecting walls had been taken away from him. They could not stay there, he was sure, though he did not know where they would go or how it would be. Soon there would be no family for him to be within; all its light would be wasted on the wide night, going up from one small flame, like the lamp on the stone table, and lost between earth and moon.

He went indoors. He called out to Dad, but his voice did not seem to penetrate the light, or overcome the noise of the saw. Dad did not look his way. The house was warm across the kitchen, cold up the stairs, and damply warm in the bedroom. He was about to sit down and take off his boots when he heard Mam, across the stairs, get up from her bed and pull the window down.

The noise of the saw came through the house. There were voices too, but the words went, like the light, everywhere but into the house. Mason thought of going through to Mam and listening with her, but instead he went downstairs again, and out of the front door.

Jedediah had come up the Incline in the darkness, and was now a black interruption to the gleam of the lamp on the rails. Dad was standing and looking down at him.

"You'll have to go, Tommy lad," Jedediah was saying. "I don't know what you have there, but if you'll let me look I'll tell you whether it will help."

"Have to go?" said Dad. "What for do I have to go?"

"You'd best be gone," said Jedediah, without any threat in his voice. "They're not going to like it when they hear."

"Hear what?" said Dad.

"When they hear that this quarry's stopping by the end of the week," said Jedediah. "It's not addling any brass; it's lossing money."

"Lossing money?" said Dad. "Since when, Jedediah? I've seen all your reports, and it's made a steady profit, plenty to keep us all going, if you weren't greedy, Jedediah."

"Some have made money, others have lost it," said Jedediah. "And maybe others have come by it."

"What does that mean?" said Dad, stepping forward with the report in his hand, pointing to it with his left one. "You've said that too often, Jedediah, and say it again and you'll sing it."

"I've said it once only," said Jedediah, "but I'll make it clear, Tommy Ross. There's money lost in the accounts that the directors haven't the right story of, and that's all I've said, and I've not said it to anyone but you, and that to your face. But there's something I've to talk to you about, Tommy. I'll come up and tell you."

"Make your way, then," said Dad, and waited for Jedediah. They both stood by the lamp. A big moth, come to the light, flew about and put smiles and scowls on their faces with its shadow. On the wall at the back of the sawing shed the shadows of the saw and its frame moved larger than the solid things themselves. On the wall of the house the shadows of Dad and Jedediah acted out some tale slightly different from the one that was being told.

"Now then," said Dad. "Who haven't you told but me?"

"What I said," said Jedediah. "There's just you that knows. And let me tell you, Tommy, that I don't believe what the books seem to say. I'm a business man, yes, but I don't think it of you, Tommy, and I can't think it of you."

"Think what, let's have the tale straight," said Dad.

"That you've made off with money that should have gone to the quarry and kept up the machines."

"You wouldn't believe that?" said Dad.

"No," said Jedediah. "But I might have to act on it, if the directors and shareholders thought it was true."

"But you don't think it's true?" said Dad.

"It doesn't matter what I think," said Jedediah. "What I think can't stop trouble coming to you, Tommy."

"Mebbe," said Dad. "Mebbe not. But I asked you, is it right you don't think I stole any money?"

"Oh, aye, right enough," said Jedediah.

"You wouldn't say so to anyone else?" said Dad.

"There's what I say, and there's what the directors say," said Jedediah. "They're mebbe not the same."

"Then what's this?" said Dad. "What's this, Jedediah Spitalhouse?" And he held before Jedediah the report Mason had brought him. Jedediah read enough of it to recognise it.

"That's not out yet," he said. "That's not public, that's not published. I don't know how you got it, but it's not been distributed."

"You don't even bloody say you don't think it's true, you don't bloody apologise," said Dad. "But you might bloody say something to this," and he hit Jedediah full in the face, not with his closed fist but with an open hand.

"That's no bloody way to fight," said Jedediah. "I'll get my bloody coat off and show you."

Dad spat. He would have spat in the fire if there had been one. Instead he spat at the lamp, and cracked the chimney so that the glass broke and fell down among the stones. The flame climbed up the air and smoked, and the light dimmed and yellowed and flickered. The giant machines on the wall bent and warped, but the real ones went on cutting slowly. The boiler of the steam engine rumbled, and started to blow steam from the safety valve.

"Give up your swearing," shouted Mam from the bedroom window. "Both of you."

"Don't you join in, Missus," Jedediah shouted back, taking off his coat and flinging it on the saw bench behind him, without noticing that the saw was working. "I've been in plenty of fights today, men and women both, and I can tackle you pair and owt else that fancies theirself."

His jacket went under the saw blade, was picked up in its teeth, and dragged up into the stone. The saw did not slow. The jacket fell away from the blade, cut in two unequal parts across sleeve and collar and back. Sliced cigars tumbled from a pocket, neat brown cylinders.

"Don't wait for him, Tommy, don't wait," shouted Mam again from the window. "Get him before he's ready. Kick him, Mason, help your Dad." Mason stood away, out of the lamp-light, at the end of the houses. Mam was like Lizzy Holmes and the rat, using words for a stick. Mason was not going to be the narrow-faced child who had helped Lizzy. Jedediah was going to be the rat, though, in its dignified aspect.

"Take no gaum," he said. "I've not heard her. This is between thee and me, Tommy. I'll use but one hand."

"Use both," said Dad. "Tha'lt need them. But aye, this is between me and thee, Jedediah. I know it does me no good, win or lose, but I've to thrash you and hang, that's all."

There was a tone in his voice that frightened Mason. There was something he had not heard before, some determination that did not care about consequence but could only see one thing to do. Perhaps Jedediah was more like the rat, because he was going to die, and perhaps Moira would have her wish and see Dad hanged.

Mason was now used to the scene. He was beginning to be able to think about what he saw, rather than receive images and impressions. He saw that battle was about to begin, that both men were looking at their ground, had stopped shouting at each other, and were talking bitterly together, about unknown matters. He felt that the scene was an eternal one, that it would go on for ever, that he had been nowhere else, and that the ending of it, if there can be an ending to eternal things, was tragic. There was too much that was tragic about him now; the whole day was encumbered with it, it dragged at every foot-step; it was not a thing of glory or heroism that went on before his eyes now but some shabby squabble. Perhaps, he thought, there are two rats, and as he thought it he knew it was a betrayal, because no one can value rats.

Thought was too much for him now. He ran away among the railway lines, into the darkness behind the sawing sheds, guilty in this same deepest betrayal, with every step and every pulse showing him and leading him into treason.

He turned once, and saw the glow of light between the house

and the sheds. There was a lifted arm between the two giant figures confronting each other in shadow on the house, titans risen from the earth. There was a moved arm, a moment later a smack of the delivered blow. Mam shouted, a screaming shout, and the shout went on and on and on. It was the valve of the engine opening a little further and releasing more steam.

Mason went behind the building where he could see nothing and went stumbling among rails and fell over the rope of the Incline. He could hear nothing now but the whistling, moaning valve: the bruising darkness that tripped and bewildered him, and the shriek on the air, were a kind of calm peace and rest.

At last he sat on the rope of the Incline, close against its top, and sobbed dry sobs without tears. Then he sat, and leaned his head against the rope, though he knew the thousand worn wires of it would touch and break and pierce his skin: hands could hold the rope but must not slide along it; heads knew no such discipline.

The rope began to send some message to him. It quivered. He thought for a moment that a truck had begun to move and was taking the rope with it. But that was not possible. Perhaps a strayed sheep was rubbing against it. Then he saw a little light down on the Incline coming closer and closer, a small flame, shining along the rope, a twisted shine, but how far off he could not tell. He looked along the rope, to see directly what it was, but the cable hung in a curve under its own weight and he looked below the light.

The light came slowly on. Mason watched it and grew more and more chilled with alarm, because of the supernatural restraint in its coming and its steadiness. Then all at once everything focussed. He saw that it was a candle, that it was not in a lantern but in the open air, that it was being carried, and the bearer of it was following the rope, touching it in order not to lose the way. And was in fact not more than fifteen feet away, and had not been more than twenty.

"Mason," said a whispered voice. "I was going away and then I heard you crying. I thought you were a sheep, or that man."

"Moira," said Mason, because he saw her clearly now. "What shall we do?"

"I don't know," said Moira, and dropped the candle. There was night again, but not a dense night. Up here there was more noise than darkness. Mason bent and picked up the candle; he had watched it fall and put his hand straight in the warm wax. They both turned their backs on the Incline and looked towards the quarry houses. There was nothing to hear but the escaping steam, nothing to see but a loom of light in the sky. Neither of them said anything about the fight.

"We'll run away," said Moira. "Where they won't know who we are."

"Yes," said Mason. He had a candle, eighteen pence, and a box of matches. That would do. Moira held his hand against her face and cried on it. He knew it was not affection, and did not want it. It was desperation. He led her across the rails, past the smithy, and out along the western edge of the quarry towards the moors above it.

XII

THE NIGHT GREW darker. Mason looked back the way they had come and saw how small the active centre was that they had left, how little was the heap of light where the fight was taking place. But his mind slipped away from the fight and thought more of the saw bevelling the stone on the saw-bed. The looking had extended his sight, and he saw that though the darkness was perhaps more the air was less dense. Close by was dark, but northwards there was light just behind the hill. Ahead there was the little wood where he had for a moment understood the world. That was not the direction to go now, because that road led up the dale where there was no way out, no places to go to, nowhere for anyone to be who would not know them.

Moira had stopped crying, and now let go of his hand. "Which is the way?" she said.

Mason led them to the land above the quarry. The skyline had been the quarry top or the slope of hill above them. Now it was the wall that bordered the road beyond, sawing the brighter sky beyond it with its row of cobblestones crowning it. There was enough light now to show through the wall where there were gaps between the stones. Mason thought that beyond it there might be a sort of day, a sort of tomorrow.

There was not. The light showed itself without coming to them. They climbed the wall in the dark, and came down into shadow on the other side too. The road showed because it was a silvery sand, but sand at night.

"Do you know where we are?" said Moira.

"Yes," said Mason. They were talking in whispers so that the night or the time would not hear. "I know this road."

"Go where we don't know," said Moira. "I don't want to be here."

The way they had come had brought them away from the noise of the steam in the safety valve. Now, perhaps because it had become louder, and perhaps because the road they were on turned back along the length of the quarry, they heard it again, pitching a tuneless note.

They walked on, silent themselves, along the straight road that did not change under their feet, with an unchanging sky far to the left, and a gathering of invisibility to the right, down the hill. The steam noise faded.

Some way ahead there was a light, small and yellow, sitting in a lump of dark. They came near enough to see that it was a light in a building, and then it went out. There was a noise in the field to the left; a goat bleated, a dog barked and dragged its chain against the reverberant wood of its kennel.

"Nanny Goat Inn," said Mason. Their legs walked on. The little cottage that was the Inn moved past them. Another yellow light showed, ahead but high. It was a star. It too went out. A dog a long way off barked at the night and then howled. Moira leaned against Mason.

"Just a dog," he said.

"Fräulein had wolves," she said.

"No," said Mason. "Not here."

"Go to where we don't know," said Moira.

They came soon to where Mason did not know. The road ended itself by running into another at a T. They could go right or left. But far to the right they heard a church clock striking and knew there must be a place there. They turned left. Moira thought she saw a wolf then, on this unfenced road, but Mason said it had horns, and that at first terrified Moira more, until she saw the creature was a sheep that walked off to find an undisturbed couch in the heather.

They went down a long slope and crossed a crooked bridge. Mason did not know where he was but thought he was not lost yet because he could have found his way home. The road began to be less sure of itself now, and there were stones to stumble on, but there was still a path that accustomed eyes could follow, and the ground was firm. They were still not wandering on the moor. There was a wall with a gap in it for a stile, and they went through that. Then they went for a long time along a shadowy lane hung over with trees and bushes. They came to a barn at the edge of a field, and sat on the stone steps of it for a time. It was cold.

"Are we lost?" said Moira. "Can we get back?"

"I don't think so," said Mason. Moira was pleased, but Mason was not sure it was right to be lost. Tomorrow, whatever happened, there was the Bank to attend. And the saw, he thought again, would still be making its way through the stone.

"There wasn't anybody left when you went," said Moira. "Nobody at all. Nobody gave me any tea."

"You could eat your dinner," said Mason. "In a bit you could have done." He remembered that it had taken him some time to eat his.

"Not at tea time," said Moira. "And nobody told me anything. Daddy didn't come back. He said he would, and he didn't. Your father kept coming to the door, but I didn't go to it always. Then Mummy came, but she wasn't any good, and it wasn't like Fräulein. Mummy can't really do things, she doesn't know what I want. Then Daddy came back and they sent me to bed and no one helped me or did anything. And the water was cold."

"I can get myself to bed," said Mason. "I don't bother washing."

"You have to if you're rich," said Moira. "Fräulein says it's seemly, but that might be a German word. Daddy and Mummy had a quarrel. They were both furious. Mummy said goodnight, but I wasn't in bed, and she went off, and Daddy went as well, and it was dark and I hadn't even a light anywhere. And there was a man outside the house, so I got the nursery candle and lit it and came out. It's got pictures on it so I didn't really want to use it, but I did, and I dropped it too. I followed Daddy, and he was being furious with your father, and I hate your mother, you know. She was my nurse once, but I still hate her. She was shouting."

"I know," said Mason. "But. Well, I don't understand why it should all be like that, Moira."

"No," said Moira. "We'll never think about it again in our whole lives. Now let's go away from everywhere."

They went away from everywhere. The lane they were in began to lose its trees on either side and to have walls instead. There was a change in the walls. They began to get higher, so that there was no light at all, except a gleam far behind them. Ahead there was nothing, on either side there was an echoing solidity, and underfoot only gravel and rock. They stopped, and wondered whether to go back to the barn, but Moira would not turn. Mason felt in his pocket and brought out the candle, struck a match, and lit the black wick. Light sizzled out from the match, crawled on the wick, then coughed and stood up. They could see the walls either side now, and the path between them, and they went on.

The walls were not only higher. The stones they were made of were larger and larger. As they went on they seemed to be growing smaller and be creeping along the roots of giant walls like the roots of mountains. Not only were the stones larger, like rocks, but the gaps between were larger too, so that they would not conceal mere insects but animals the size of a fox, or a wolf. Then cows could be hidden, and surely a wall with gaps large enough to let cows through could have no use in the English countryside.

"We've got littler," said Mason.

Moira drew in her breath, because the air had not grown different. "Good," she said. She wanted to be in an unreachable place, and to be a hundred times smaller than the rest of mankind was to be in a different world. But she wanted time to consider. "Let's not go any further," she said. "Wait a bit."

"Too cold to stop," said Mason. "It's cold enough walking with the candle because we can't go so fast."

"There's pictures on it," said Moira. "We can go a bit more far if you want."

They went a bit more far. Moira said she smelt spiders and began to look round for things the size of tigers. Mason thought the smell was sheep and there, between two of the giant stones, was a little sheep-fold. There were no sheep in it. Mason remembered a story about some sailors in a cave with a one-eyed giant and some sheep, on an island. It was possible, he thought, and looked upward. There was stone overhead as well as round about.

"Dead sheep," said Moira, looking at the bundled corpses stacked at one side of the fold. But the bundles were not corpses; they were the rolled-up fleeces of the sheep that had recently been here, and held most of the smell. Moira saw what they were too.

"We could sit on them," she said. She sat against the heap, and partly sank into it, and dislodged some of them. Mason pulled some of the bundles out and made a couch of them for her and she lay on them. Then he undid a fleece, because he knew how they were folded, and laid it like a blanket over Moira, putting the clean neck-end next to her face.

"Not fancy," he said, "but grand happings."

"Warm," said Moira, and closed her eyes, opened them, and could not keep them open. Mason pulled himself out a couch and a cover, and put himself to bed. He was not going to sleep, but to watch over Moira and rest his legs and his back while he did so. He put out the candle and saved it in his pocket again. He thought for a time that he could still see the walls and roof of the place where he was but it was imagination, because when he closed his own eyes he still saw the glimmer within himself that the candle flame left.

He stayed awake for a little time, finding himself uncomfortable. He still had on his suit and high collar. He pulled his tie off and unclipped the collar from its studs and laid it beside him. He went to sleep immediately though he knew it was happening and fought it. He hoped only to be in a swoon of sleep while his eyes stretched themselves. But his waking was from deep down and he had dreamed of the saw in the lamplight. He found his mouth dry and that he had been snoring. He licked his mouth sensible again, tasting the sheep now. He was warm and comfortable and knew where he was, or if not quite that, he knew how he had got where he was. He thought of Moira, for no reason that he knew, and remembered that she was here, that they had come here and grown smaller on the way, and that all they had done was irretrievable, they had left home and this was what had happened to them. He sat up, remembering that he had meant to watch.

There was light but no colour. The air was cold outside the fleece. Moisture had formed over him and his hand was wet when he laid it on his leg. But inside the wool he was dry. Moira lay sleeping soundlessly.

Mason felt there was an urgency about something and that activity was called for. There was something wrong, he knew. He settled, in a little while, that he was in bed with his boots on, and that once they were off he would be forgiven and all would be well. He undid the laces, pulled the boots off, put his feet under the fleece again, and went to sleep once more.

The next time he woke there was a mist round him, with the sense of warm light somewhere above. He saw plainly now that he was not in a cave, but only under the overhang of an enormous stone, which touched the one next to it without joining it. They were in a crack in the side of the wall, not in a cave. He could see round him only huge stones, as if he and Moira were inside the base of the wall, but cloaking the stones was the mist, not moving, he thought, but getting thicker and thinner in patches. He sat up, awake. Moira had turned a little but was fast asleep.

Moira, he thought. Moira. She would have to be taken back. They both had to go back. It came to him as a thought that there was really nowhere to go but to their own families. Then that thought was overwhelmed by the idea that they had got beyond being able to return, that they were in some condition for which there was no remedy. Either they had grown small, or they were in a place where things were impossibly big. The giant might claim them.

Mason found himself believing anything, even that he was at home dreaming. But he was being now; this was where he was, and this was where Moira was. He got up from his couch and stood in his stockinged feet in the light ancient dung of sheep. The cold mist touched him and woke him. He walked out of the fold. It had been formed by the large stones, and the gaps between filled with other unshaped fragments. The entrance was a wooden gate. He went out into the path beyond, where there was heather, and tufts of bilberry plants making cushions between the heather and the rocks.

He followed the path upwards, towards the light overhead. The mist began to lessen as he went up, but once he stopped and hesitated because a ghostly rock barred his way. It was the shadow of a real one. Beyond it he came into low sunshine. It was bright here, and more than bright. There was a dazzle like metal.

He shaded his eyes with their lashes and his brow. The sunshine warmed him. It struck back at him as light from a long level of cloud, lying flat as far as he could see on all sides, ending somewhere that he could not identify, in a far blue cloud or strange circle of surrounding hill.

Stranger objects than merely unknown ones were closer at

hand. Out of the level plain of mist, or balanced on it, were more huge stones, or rocks, scattered randomly, so still and silent and brooding and watchful that they must be alive. Only living things could keep themselves so detached, support themselves on this sea of air. They were real enough; they cast shadows. And there were others swimming just below the surface, showing now and then and plunging away again. It was all in a quiet unmatched by anything Mason had known. He knew it was some new world he had come to, that now there was no return to the quarry and the town and the Bank. Perhaps they were the dream. There was no way of telling.

The rocks stopped looking at him. He looked at them instead. He knew they were not alive, since he stood close by one, and it had a familiar rough earthly licheny surface. But of course other planets are made of stone.

A bird went up out of the mist. He heard its wing without seeing it. He heard it begin its song, going further and further away with it and losing no intensity. The sound fell like arrows into the mist, and not only fell but radiated in every direction from the bird, so that Mason felt the whole universe visible to him was full of the sound of one creature. As it had been with the bones of the rabbit in the wood, so it was now. He began to understand more than the world he knew; the meaning of existence came clear to him. There were no words, or shapes, or sounds to the understanding. Here he was witnessing the fitting together of fragments so that the angle was right, of surface and mark so that the drawing lived. The world of sight and sound was about to take him up into its beauty when the balance changed.

There was another noise, pulling him back uncountable miles

of thought, whole centuries of contemplation. There was a strange vibrant wailing down below in the mist. He recognised it. It was Moira's voice. She had woken and found herself alone, and was crying and calling for someone to come to her.

The vision he had been having, without changing at all, stopped being charged with electrical magic and became only an unusual scene. He turned from it, because he knew it had slipped away for ever, and went down the path to the sheepfold.

Moira's crying had only been a practice. There were no tears yet. But she had been frightened to find herself alone, and now was about to be angry.

"Isn't there anyone else?" she said. "I'm cold again." She had sat up but since the fleeces had flattened under her she was down on the ground. "Where are we? I want to know now."

"I don't know where we are," said Mason. "But it's sunny out there, if you want to come and look."

"Yes I do," said Moira. "Mason, I'm dreadfully hungry. I never had any dinner or tea yesterday."

"We could go on home," said Mason. "I think."

"No," said Moira. "Never."

"Come and look up here then," said Mason. "It's beautiful."

Moira humped herself up from her couch and shook the wool from her. She ran her fingers through her hair. "I'm a fright," she said.

"You look all right," said Mason, but he slightly grudged having to say it and found he could not say the other thing he wanted to say, that she was pretty, because it sounded less than the beautiful he had called the sunshine and mist. But the sunshine and mist were perhaps the most beautiful sight he had seen, with the added enchantment that had been upon them.

She came up to the top of the little path with him, and stood against the same rock and looked at the same things and heard that bird lofting its song.

"I think we've died," she said. "This can't be anywhere. And I can't be hungry in paradise, can I?"

"No," said Mason. "But I think I can."

"Yes," said Moira. "It is beautiful, though. But we don't know where it is, do we?"

"It's like looking inside ourselves," said Mason, because the enchantment of it crept over him once more for a time, then retreated.

"That's where Heaven is," said Moira. "Inside you. But Fräulein wouldn't let me in with hair like this, Mason."

A crow came flying across the mist, thoughtfully, like a black albatross, looking from side to side as it came. It saw them, and banked away, and grew smaller and smaller and went out of sight. They both laughed at its demeanour, and decided that this was not Heaven since for some reason it would be impossible for crows to be there.

They went back to the sheepfold, meaning to stack the fleeces where they had been and walk on. But Moira tidied her couch and went to sleep on it again. Mason did the same to his, lay down and contemplated the vision he had had.

For a time he thought new visions had set in. But he had woken from a dreamy sleep into broad daylight. The mist had gone and the sunshine was slanting down among the rocks. He could not tell what time it was, but he felt as broadly awake as the daylight, and only normally hungry.

Moira woke when he was packing his fleeces away.

"We stink," he said. "Like shepherds."

"Like sheep," said Moira. "Fräulein would be quaint about it."

They went out of the place they had been in. Mason went to the top of the path. By daylight, with the mist lifted, the sight was just as extraordinary. The rocks that had seemed to float were the pinnacles of even vaster, taller rocks that stood all round them on a high stretch of moorland, congregated like ancient animals that had turned to stone among chapels and statues, temples and friezes, jutting bergs, distorted pudding-shapes thirty feet tall, heaps like grains of black salt nine feet across, slabs balanced on slabs, layer tipped against layer, all in grey gritty stone. They were alone in it, even more alone than when the mist had lifted them up into the silver of nowhere. Mason could see beyond the rocks now. Down where the crow had flown was the distant mass of Green Hill, and to the right of that the unmistakable shape of the head of the dale. And on the right shoulder of the hill was the quarry chimney, three miles away, that carried the smoke of the sawing-shed engine.

Mason could take them home in less than an hour. "Where shall we go?" he said.

"Home," said Moira. "There isn't anywhere else."

XIII

MASON FASTENED UP his collar. His neck was sticky and the collar stuck to it and was uncomfortable beyond bearing. But he tied his tie and left it slack and then undid the front stud and let the tie hold the collar further away from his skin.

They were down in the shaded lane now between hedges grown high. The morning sun did not come here at all, and it was cold. Mason's arm tickled, or worse than tickled; something seemed to be drilling gently into a fold of skin at his armpit, sending feathers of sensation down his side. He took a good scratch at it, clenching his teeth together to get a better purchase. Something did much the same thing to Moira, and she scratched at her wrist, then at her leg.

"You go on," she said. "I'm going to take my stockings off. I think there's hay-seeds got under my garters."

Mason went on. Now he was finding the same hay-seeds jabbing at his waist. He pulled his shirt up, now he was alone, and saw that something had bitten him four or five times round the waist under the elastic of his underpants. There were no hay-seeds, and hay-seeds do not bite. There would have been something in the fleeces, perhaps, something used to sheep.

"Heat bumps," said Moira, coming up trailing her stockings. "They always hurt most in the cold weather. If it gets cold when it's been hot."

"It's lops off the sheep," said Mason. "I think they drop off in a bit." Then one bit him hard inside his elbow and he turned to beat at the place. He was angry now with what bit him, and he was able to wish Moira was not there and that he could throw off his jacket and shirt and search for fleas. He remembered what the creatures were called.

"Sheep keds," he said. "That's what we've got."

"Nasty," said Moira. "Having things on you. Is my face dirty? It feels nasty."

"It isn't right clean," said Mason. "I think it's clarped up with grease off the wool."

"My fingers stick together," said Moira. "And look." She put a hand up to the dewed leaves of a hanging tree and let the drops run into her palm. The drops stood up in a blister, trying to get away from the waxed skin. When she rubbed her hands together the blister did not flatten but broke into thirty pieces, all separate striving blisters. She shook her hand and the water fell away. Mason dipped his hand into a trickle of water that ran through the grass beside the lane. The hand came out dry.

"Did I scratch your face?" said Moira.

"You did that," said Mason. "I'm scratched worse now and I did all the new scratches, off these keds." He knew she had scratched him, but the reason did not come to mind.

"Yesterday," said Moira. Mason thought about yesterday, and it was a long way off, not so much in time as in its relationship to him. He was surprised to find that the recollection of it was part of his own memory. It was almost as if he had been remembering things for someone else, not part of his own experience. Nothing altered the first strange fact of today, that he was here, walking home from running away with Moira, or not running away quite, but leaving all the yesterdays.

But now they were coming back to the yesterdays. They were walking along the path that was turning to road over the moor. A mile or so ahead was the Nanny Goat Inn. Somewhere beyond that, and not very far beyond, he would have to give Moira back to Jedediah. He was glad that it would be someone else's turn for her.

That was more betrayal, more treason, he thought. Last night he had betrayed his own family by leaving it; now he was betraying his own love by being not interested any more. He wondered how it was possible to feel indifferent, to wish just a little that Lizzy Holmes was there instead, a little more vital and energetic than Moira, who was walking slowly and carelessly, dragging her shoe toes on the ground, scratching with an idle hand at her side, and beginning to moan about the long distance.

Mason abandoned all females, and wondered whether Lantho might not be the best company he could have.

"I'm so hungry," said Moira. "My chest feels hollow. My breath goes in all cold. I'm sorry I scratched you, Mason."

"I hit you first," said Mason. He remembered why he had hit her; it had been on a hope of hanging for Dad. He wondered whether the fight would end in hanging for both Dad and Jedediah, but he felt there was something wrong with the sense of that. Now, by daylight, he could not think that the fight had started at all, and he knew there could be no end. They would stop fighting, and nothing would be changed.

The sun was shining, he was going home. He had looked at rocks floating and heard celestial singing. That was all enough. There were keds biting him, but keds are better than love.

Now Moira was crying. He asked why, supposing he could not ever understand. She was crying for everything, she said; for coming away, for being hungry, for going home, for Fräulein, for Mummy, for scratching Mason's face, for Daddy fighting among the rails. She had to sit down, pale and tearful, by the side of the road, until she stopped gulping.

Mason thought that he liked her, but his heart did not turn over. Was it possible to stop loving?

"I'll help you along," he said. Then he tried an experiment with truth, to see whether there was any current in the affectionate wire of his mind, whether his tongue could be a switch to turn things on again.

"I love you," he said.

"I love you when you aren't there," said Moira.

"That's what I mean too," said Mason, and it was true though not the whole truth.

Moira put a hand up for him, and they clasped waxy fingers and walked on, to the place where the road to the quarry top joined, where they had heard the church strike from far away. Here Moira found she had lost a stocking. They looked back and left it where it was, somewhere out of sight.

The road was straight but went over the curve of the hill. Ahead of them someone else walked, in sight for a moment and then over the far side of some dip or rise. Mason thought it was Lantho with his bag of papers under his arm; there was a sort of loping stride a little one-sided that Lantho had. But he went off the road somewhere, whoever it was.

The Nanny Goat Inn was on the right. The goats were wideawake now and came to the end of the field to look at them as they passed and call. The dog called back to the goats from the far side of the house.

The Inn was a tiny cottage. Here you could get not only ale but milk: for it Fräulein came on Sundays sometimes, stepping no doubt across quarrymen who had too much headache to have heard a sermon at all.

"We could get some milk," said Mason.

"Are there any quarrymen?" said Moira. Mason looked over the wall, and saw none lining the path or covering the grass with bursting brows. There was no money for ale these days.

The dog made most welcome, barking wildly and wagging its tail wildly at the same time, and contriving to tattoo with its chain as if it had music set before it.

"You walk into hotels," said Moira.

"This isn't really like one," said Mason. He tapped at the door. The dog said that the end of the world was here, to the people inside, wake up and repent. It became so frantic to leave its chain that it turned its back on Mason and Moira and pulled its collar half over its head. They could see the round bones behind its ears.

A window opened above and a woman shouted at the dog. It went into its kennel and lay against the back wall, shouting in muffled tones that it told them so and they wouldn't listen.

The door opened and the Innkeeper's wife looked at them. "You're soon here," she said. "Too young for ale, too young."

"Mebbe some milk," said Mason.

"Too old for milk," she said. "Too old. Come away, then, and you'll have some, by-like." Then she shouted: "Bacca, out and milk the black nanny; there's a lady and gentleman in a collar wanting some." She had not turned her head away when she shouted, or opened her mouth any wider, only made more noise. Now she spoke again. "Sit again the table," she said. "Bacca won't be so long."

Bacca came down, pulling on his trousers and went outside, where the dog was glad to see him and sang a hymn about it. His wife raked at the fire, threw some candle-ends on it, where they fired in the hot blackness and smoked a greasy smoke, and dropped a match in the smoke. It began to blip and burn.

Mason slumped on the wooden settle. Its back pressed on his bones, but he would have dreamed wideawake if the keds had not begun their testing bites again.

"Shepherds, are you? Shepherds?" asked the woman.

"No," said Moira. "We are just on the way home."

"Then you must be sheep," said the woman. "Sheep," and she laughed. "Nothing ever smelt more like a shepherd than a sheep, and you're one or the other," and she went on without pausing, "Bacca, look sharp, they want to sup it, not take the cheeses home. The old fool," she added in her normal voice. "Old."

Bacca came in shortly with a bowl of milk. Then he drew himself a mug of ale from a barrel in the corner and sat by the fire to drink it. The woman strained the milk through a cloth, dipped two more mugs into it, and pushed them milky across the table. The milk was warm, fresh, and tasted of animals. They had two mugs each, and then sat on the settle warm and full while the woman sat on a stool the far side of the fire and studied them.

"I make nowt of you," she said. "Nowt. Too young for one thing, too old for another, too few or too many. You're true folk, are you? Will you pay?"

"My daddy will pay," said Moira. "He will send the money up."

"It's sixpence," said the woman. "And who's your Daddy, lass? Who?"

"Mr Spitalhouse," said Moira.

"No, lass," said the woman. "Not Jedediah Spitalhouse. He'll never pay. He hasn't sixpence to his name, nor three-pence either, nor a penny piece."

"He has a lot of money," said Moira. "I have enough. I have about thirteen pounds."

"Twelve thirteen six," said Mason, reeling off the pounds, shillings and pence of her bank book. He had often looked at it, and had written the last entry himself.

"The six will fit," said the woman. "And it's more likely."

By now Mason had brought out sixpence of his own and laid it on the table. The woman took it and put it on the shelf over the fire. Bacca tipped up his ale mug and looked at them as they went. The dog said he was glad to see them again, and watch me go behind my kennel and chase it into the next field among the goats, and never mind about the end of the world, that was yesterday and we missed it.

"It is a mad dog," said Moira, running to the gate, not because she was frightened of it but because she was full of milk and happy again. "My milk slops inside me."

The dog stood on its hind legs at the full length of its chain and said a prayer towards them. Then it sat down and distinctly laughed.

"They give it ale, that's what," said Mason. "I've heard of it."

"Do they give it to the goats?" said Moira. "I feel all strange; all the milk is in my arms."

Mason wondered whether the goats had been having ale too, and it had been in the milk. He and Moira ran down the road now, and missed the gate that should have taken them into the quarry, and went on down the hill until they came to the little wood, and had to turn back. Now Mason noticed that the steam engine was quiet, or at least the valve on it was not blowing. When they turned about and came towards the quarry again they saw that the tall chimney was smoking. Mason said nothing, but it proved to him that Dad was all right and still there. No one else would have tended the fire so early. He did not know the time, in fact, but it felt like seven o'clock.

They were walking along below the quarry, between it and Bishopside Hall, because Mason knew that if it were round seven o'clock there might be blasting at the quarry face. He thought of Mam coming to his room and finding his unslept-in bed, with just the mark where he had sat for a moment before going out again. Now she would be missing him, but in a moment they would be home.

Then he knew there would be blasting, because there was a spluttering on the bare slope of the fresh tip above them, and down it wandered the puffing trail of a piece of fuse. Moira was startled at it, as if it were a snake. It was an unknown thing to her, hissing among the stones.

"It's all right," said Mason. "It's not alive. The shot-firer throws away bits of fuse and burns them up so he doesn't use

163

them again, because they aren't any good if he's had them out. I can get a bit and show you one day."

They went on. Moira looked back at it. They had stepped over it where it was unburnt. It was then that Moira noticed she had lost the second stocking, but she did not care about that either.

There was no blast in the quarry yet. Mason thought it must be well before seven still. They came out on to the Incline a little below its top, where it was steepest, where Mason had been sitting in the dark the night before. The chimney beyond was standing under its smoke. They crossed the Incline and its slack cable, and went up the other side of it, and on to the top among the rails.

There was no one about now. There was smoke from the house, but the door was shut and the windows shut too. It must be well before seven.

"I should go home," said Moira. "I'll just run on down."

"Wait on," said Mason. "Let's ask Mam what happened."

Moira followed him. They went round to the back door. Mason opened it and went in. Moira said she would stop there for now.

"No, it'll be right, come in," said Mason. He went in himself, having been away seven years at least. Nothing was changed, though; he knew the smell of the place. But there was a difference. There was the smell of a cigar. Mason remembered that Jedediah's cigars had been cut in two the night before by the now quiet saw. But burning cuts a cigar in two anyway, so perhaps they could be started halfway down. And a cigar smoked meant Jedediah.

Mason went through the middle room and to the kitchen.

Mam was there. Dad was there. Drinking tea with them was Jedediah. Dad had a red nose. Jedediah had a black eye.

"By gum, Mason, you're up," said Mam. "I forgot to call you. Here's your breakfast ready. You'll have to get yourself a pie in the village for your dinner, Jedediah's eaten all the bread."

"Oh, yes," said Mason, and last night had not happened, it was a dream. He had not been missed. "Has Jedediah been here?"

"Aye," said Jedediah. "And . . ."

The front door rattled under a heavy banging. Mam went to it, saying something about quarrymen coming at all hours. It was not a quarryman at the door but Lantho, and under his arm was the bag that he carried papers in.

"Morning Mrs Ross," he said. "Is your husband in? I'd just like to have a talk with him."

"At his breakfast, Marrick Lantho," said Mam. "Come in."

Lantho came in, as near to smiling broadly as he ever got. Then the folds of the smile went away suddenly. He had seen Jedediah.

"Spitalhouse," he said. "I thought you were in Leeds. For God's sake, is there anyone in your house? I thought you'd left."

"Aye," said Jedediah, dropping his cigar. "There's our lass. Why?"

Lantho dropped his bag that held papers, turned towards the door, pulled it open and ran out of the house.

"What's up with him?" said Jedediah, nearly sitting back and reaching for the dropped cigar.

Moira had heard him talking and had followed Mason

through. Dad had gone out of the door after Lantho who shouted from outside, and Dad shouted something back towards the house. Jedediah heard what it was, and jumped up from his chair, knocking the table crooked as he went so that plates and knives and the milk jug tottered and fell to the floor. He elbowed Mam aside and got next out of the door. Mam was after him, with her hands in her apron, not knowing whether to tend the table or the rout going on outside.

Jedediah shouted some word back to her, but she did not understand it, and stood hesitating on the stone outside the door. Mason and Moira stood with her, and then took infection of the chase and ran after Jedediah. Lantho was out of sight now, round the end of the sawing shed, going towards the Incline. When Mason and Moira came to the top of the Incline Lantho was halfway down it, running in the long grass, stumbling and picking himself up. Dad was after him, and Jedediah beside Dad, running down inside the track between the ropes. The brakeman was watching them go and shaking his head, because of the danger of running on the Incline when the trucks were moving, as they were now. The first load was dropping, and the rope was tight. The wooden rollers were groaning as the rope ground over them. The big wheel at the far end of the top siding groaned too, with the brake-blocks rubbing on its rim.

"Now you bairns," said the brakeman, but he did not stop Mason and Moira, who were following the men, though they did not know why.

"Lantho thinks you're there," said Mason.

"That's the man," said Moira. "I think he was there."

Lantho was going to Bishopside Hall. At the gate on the side

166

of the Incline he went out of sight. A hundred yards behind was Dad. At the gate he stopped for a moment and waved Jedediah back, but Jedediah came on. Dad had just gone through the gate when Bishopside Hall was blown up by four separate explosions that ran into one in their echoes and went on again and again among the hills. There was a moving in the air and Mason stopped running. Jedediah stopped too, and bent double and breathed heavily, unable to go any further. Against the background of echo of the explosions came the rattle of falling debris. Pieces of stone and wood came flying viciously through the air and landed embedded in the ground. Among the trees beside the Incline there grew a dusty cloud, perhaps of smoke, and beyond and beside the dust there was a place where nothing stood where the house had been. In the dust stone and wood and metal still tumbled.

"Dad," said Mason. Dad came walking shakily out of the gate, and up the Incline towards Jedediah.

"They," said Mason. "They think you are in there." Then he sat down in the grass and was gently sick of all the milk he had drunk. Moira held his hand. "I'm all right," he said, not at all repelled by what was happening and then had happened and was over. "It wasn't nasty."

"It was just windies," said Moira. "Like babies have. Come on."

Mason went down with her, wiping his mouth on his sleeve. He was still bothered most in the world by keds, and whether Mam had a clean collar for him to go to work in.

XIV

MOIRA WAS PATTING Jedediah on the back, as if he too had wind like a baby. What he had was the opposite, breathlessness. He responded by holding Moira with one hand and pushing her away with the other, wanting her and repelling her.

"What's going off?" he said, gasping. "You stink of sheep shit."

"Give over, Daddy," said Moira.

Jedediah sat down. He drew in a shuddering breath and let it flow out again. "Cigars," he said. "I'm off them now; they leave you with nothing worth breathing." His face was red in places, white in others, and a blue bruise lay round his eye, where there was a swelling that blueness would creep into later.

The rope of the Incline went almost silently by. From it there came, as if unpeeling from the coiled wire, a thread of sound that was the axle and wheel noise of the truck rising and falling and the muffling of the brake on the big wheel in the quarry.

Mr Ross walked up from the gate of Bishopside Hall.

"We'll have to go in," he said. "Mason, you'd better run on down to Dr Connaught and tell him to be along."

"She wasn't in, Tommy," said Jedediah, putting his arm round Moira's knees.

"He didn't know that," said Dad, indicating with his head

the ruin beyond the wood that had been Bishopside Hall. "He must have been in there."

"Moira wasn't," said Jedediah. "Other folk didn't need to be."

"Aye, but," said Dad.

"Aye but and all," said Jedediah. "Never mind, happen. There's plenty of folk coming that'll look in there in a minute, Tommy. Better we don't go near, I think."

The noise of the explosions had brought people from their houses in the village. Now they had had time to get to the bottom of the Incline and to the bridge over it, the road going towards Bishopside Hall. They came in ones and twos and then as a crowd, some pushing up the Incline some going along the road.

The gate that led to the Hall opened and shut. The four of them on the Incline looked. Lantho had opened it and closed it and come through. He was covered in dust and the lining of his jacket showed through in several places, and there was a knee visible. One hand was to his head.

He spoke to them, but at that moment the descending truck was beside them and the mutter of its wheels covered Lantho's words.

"Wait on," said Dad. "I'll get him, he's knocked dizzy. Wait on, Lantho." Lantho went on talking through Dad's shouts.

"Deafed," said Jedediah. "It's deafed him, being so near."

Lantho had not heard. He did not hear the ascending wagon close behind him, singing its imperturbable quiet song with its hollow burden. He did not hear the shouts of warning from Dad and Jedediah. Mason thought they need not have shouted, because it was only the empty wagon, coming up the hill, and there was no great weight with it. Men down on the dock, or up at the quarry, could move an empty wagon alone. He had forgotten the long taut loop of the wire cable, joining the many tons in the other wagon to this light one, making it equal in deadly power. The corner of the wagon came up and touched Lantho, pushing him over. He reached for the closest thing, the cable, touched it and let go, raising his arms like the dog at the Nanny Goat Inn at the end of its chain half an hour before. He was brought down by the wagon. It passed over him, undisturbed. Then it stopped. The brakeman had seen something happen, and put on the brake.

As they all came to Lantho, and found him lying dead in his own spilled calm blood, the whistle at the building above began to blow its short blasts of alarm.

"There'll be no hurry," said Jedediah. "He didn't deserve that, didn't Lantho. But he's done what I couldn't do, Tommy. Now Lantho," he said, addressing the body, "you've done a daft thing, and it was to pay for, one way and another, for they'd have caught you and locked you up."

"Would you have let them?" said Moira. Now she was pulling away from the scene, holding Jedediah not Mason. She had looked only once towards Lantho, without blinking, and understood all in that moment about his dying. She had looked away and was ready to go away.

"Not for me to say," said Jedediah. "That's a police job, aye, and there he is coming, is the bobby. Lantho, you did a good turn there, and you'll be thanked yet."

"It's our house," said Moira. "What's good about that? I want to go and see."

"I was wanting rid," said Jedediah. "Aye, Tommy, it had come to that; there's not enough brass in me, that's it. I was wanting rid, and no one would take it, they wouldn't look. But this way there'll be the insurance money, and that'll clear us."

The policeman was coming up the Incline now. He had pushed his way through the gathering, creeping crowd, told off a man to keep them back, and came up alone.

The brakeman came down from the quarry, now he had stopped blowing the alarm whistle. He was giving a hand to Mam, bringing her bundle of clean linen rags. He was carrying two chocks to wedge the two trucks on the line.

Behind the policeman came another uniformed figure, with his sack. The postman was coming. Down in the village the train came to the station, bringing its bank of cloud.

"I've to get to the Bank," said Mason. "But I can't get in without I've the key."

"Then stop where you are," said Dad. "Stop where you are anyroad, while the bobby gets here."

Mam and the brakeman were there before the policeman. The brakeman chocked the wagon that had killed Lantho, went past him, and said: "It's none so easy to see from yonder; I just watch to see the rope isn't going over-fast, that's how I tell mostly." Then he went on to the lower wagon.

Mam came with the bundle and touched Lantho. She did not open the bundle.

"Now then, Mr Spitalhouse," said the policeman, when he came up. "What is it?" But he could see very well that they were waiting beside Lantho. "Can you cover him up?" he said.

Mam undid the bundle. There was in the middle of it one

171

piece that was not torn but hemmed neatly all round. She spread it over the body and it was no longer with them in the detached way it had been before, Lantho without Lantho, but greatly and horridly present, Lantho with death, death with the dead. Mason's heart went dry. From the crowd at the bottom of the Incline there came a changed sigh now that they knew something positive.

"He stepped in the way of the wagon," said Dad. "It over-ran him. That empty one." The policeman went to look.

"There'll be statements," said the policeman, "from those that saw it. But there's more than that, I doubt."

"What you came up for last time," said Dad. "Solved, mebbe."

They all waited, because the postman had come up the Incline and approached Jedediah. His eyes were really on the shrouded figure between the rails. "I've a registered letter to sign for, Mr Spitalhouse," he said. "Who's yon? A quarry-man?"

"Lantho," said Jedediah. "Give me the slip and a pencil; I've nowt with me."

"I heard a crack along the road," said the postman. "And by gum, I thought, when I came up your drive, by gum, I'll go to sea, there's no house left, and there wasn't. Blown up, was it? Blown up eh."

"Aye," said Jedediah. He had signed the slip and gave it back. The postman handed him a letter with blue lines round it. Jedediah slid it into his hip pocket.

"Owt for the top?" said Dad. "You're that close."

"There will be," said the postman. "In the bottom of the bag."

172

He went to the bottom of the sack and came out with the letters for the quarry office and any private ones for Dad.

"I tell you what," said Jedediah, "I'll take those and all, Tommy, if you don't mind. You'll not want to be reading them."

"No?" said Dad.

"Nay," said Jedediah. "There's been a change here since that happened."

Mam had done up her bundle. Dad handed the letters to Jedediah. Mam gave the bundle to Mason, and went across to Moira. "Come on, you bairns," she said. "I think we'll do better at home now, my home I mean. Come on, Mason."

"Aye, take them," said the policeman. "Mr Spitalhouse, we'd best get to the Hall and keep folk out of there. We don't know what's left to fire in there."

Mam and Moira were waiting for Mason. But now he thought that he was of the active man's world, and should stay where things were still going on. He told Mam he would be up later. They went up the slope. Mason watched the next person coming up from below.

It was Dr Connaught. He looked at Lantho, said there was nothing he could do, that it was obvious the wagon had killed him but that he might have died in any case from the explosion, and what the devil had he been blowing up, the whole powder shed?

Out of curiosity he stayed, and went with them through the gate into the grounds of Bishopside Hall. Here there were stones that had been bowled over the grass. Taller flowers and shrubs had been laid flat by the general force of the blast. The house itself had burst and the stones had separated and then fallen down. Here and there some internal part had spurted outwards and household things were scattered outside it. Some kitchen affairs lay in broken blue china on a gravel walk. The light-shy wallpaper of the drawing room stood in the sun, on a wall that had not fallen, and on a piece that had. The low wing that had been the nursery was ripped open like a doll's house and was full of its own debris. A scrap-book moved its bright ill-arranged pages among broken budding roses.

"There was a long fuse on it," said Dad. "Lantho was in our house a minute before."

"It was him," said Jedediah.

"He'd have a grudge, still?" said the policeman. "Would that be it?"

"About Eileen?" said Jedediah. Eileen was the Irishwoman's name. "No, not by now. He was a strange fellow anyroad, was Lantho. And he wasn't aiming to kill me. When he came in Tommy's house up there he saw me, and he said he thought I was in Leeds, and he came on down here because I said the little lass was in here."

"But she wasn't," said the policeman. "Or she'd mebbe stepped out."

"She was in the house up there, our house," said Mason. "She was with me."

"I thought you were in bed?" said Dad. "I never heard you get up."

"I never went to bed," said Mason. "And Moira didn't, because she didn't want to be in her house alone. We went for a walk, because . . ."

"Aye," said Jedediah. "We weren't good company last night, I think, and we were better left."

"Well, that's something else," said Dad. "Nowt to do with this."

"It has and it hasn't," said Jedediah. "But I'll get it all straight in a bit."

"We saw the fuse," said Mason. "It was up there, under the tips, the way we came back. We saw it burning. I thought it must be an old bit the shot-firer had thrown out. We came that way because we didn't know the time and they might have been blasting. It was burning, but I never thought about anything else being at the end of it."

The shot-firer was at the other side of the debris. He had been studying the wreckage with a professional eye. He reckoned that the amount of explosive used about matched up to the amount missing from the powder house.

There was a tiny hand under some roof slates. Mason bent and picked it up. It was the pot hand of a doll, with a pot wrist and then part of the fore-arm. Stitched to it was a cloth elbow and upper arm, and further under the stone was the rest of Loosan. Her cloth body was not torn but in some way the weave had opened out and the sawdust evaporated from it. The silken scar had held a part together. Under the open weave there was the shape and glitter of a coin. Mason picked it out. It was a German coin, of five pfennigs. He covered Loosan again. Somewhere near would lie Betty, Florence, Minta, Daisy, Jecka, Hildy, and Lorly. He did not look.

They went back to the Incline. Mason asked the policeman about the key to the Bank. The policeman said he thought it would be all right to take it from Lantho, and did it himself. The key was still warm when Mason took it. The ambulance men came and said they would take the body down to the workhouse, where the morgue was, since they were here and had a stretcher.

"Wait on," said Jedediah. "Here's Eileen."

The Irishwoman had come through the crowd, gone along as far as the Hall and looked at the fallen house. Now she came up the edge of the grounds and through the gate. No one offered to show her Lantho, but she came and looked, pulling back the cloth that covered him. The ambulance men pulled it right off a moment later and put his own cloth there instead. Dad took Mam's cloth, folded in its own folds, because Lantho had not stirred any of them, though he had made other marks.

"Where's my daughter, Jedediah, that you've let this happen?" said the Irishwoman.

"She's right enough," said Jedediah. "She's up in the quarry. Mary's got her."

"I'll be there, then," said the Irishwoman, and she went on, first holding out her hand for the shroud, which Dad was holding and wishing he was not, because he wanted his hand free. The Irishwoman turned. "One of you be sending for a prayer to be said for him," she called. "Whoever he might have been if I had chosen, Jedediah Spitalhouse."

The Irishwoman went up the Incline. Lantho went down. Jedediah stood and looked at the ground, thinking. Mason thought he might be considering how he was related in time and experience to the Irishwoman and Lantho. He might have thought of that, but perhaps he only thought about what he was soon to say. Mason looked at himself and scratched at a ked bite. He was looking at the ground too, but mostly so that he did not stare at Lantho's carry. Lantho came down to the crowd and it parted before him, and changed in aspect, becoming whiter as caps were lifted from bald heads, and darker as faces bent down in a moment of something like prayer. Mason was waiting to go down himself, and to his desk, but not the company of someone who should have been there too.

"I'll want statements," said the policeman. "You'd better come in when you've got your work going, Mr Ross, Mr Spital-house. It's all to be reported."

"We'll do that," said Jedediah. "Let them come up, will you? I want to speak to them."

Jedediah went down the Incline a little way and climbed up on to the laden wagon, and stood on the stone in it. The police-man went down to the crowd and released them with a word, then turned towards the Hall, to keep people away from there.

Men and women came up the Incline. Jedediah put his hand up to gather them round where he was, but a lot of them went to look where Lantho had lain before coming to Jedediah. Dad said he would be off, but Jedediah leaned down and restrained him.

"Now folk, listen," he said. The people jostled for a moment and then listened. "There's a man dead that shouldn't be dead. It's my fault, and you can put the blame on me. There was a man hurt not many weeks since, that shouldn't have been, and that's my fault too."

"I's right enough now," said the man, out of the crowd, "and doing as well on sickness benefit as on the dole."

"Happen," said Jedediah. "But there's many out of work that ought not to be, and that's to do with me and all."

There were calls of denial when he said that, but Jedediah stopped them. "Nay," he said. "I know. I know about it all.

I've been in a wealthy way for a few years now, and there's no doubt of it, I've had some brass come my way. And I've had some brass leave me and all. But you know I was born in this town, and I live here yet, or I did while I had my house. I bought up most of the quarry, there's just a few shares I never got hold of. I pay expenses of it, and I pay the wages. And I get the profits, most of them. But these last six or seven years I've not had a penny out of here that I've been able to keep, because there's not the profit there was, and when I did have a good year I'd to put the money in other places because there'd been a bad year there. If I'd been a right keen business man I'd have got rid of this quarry years since, got out of the village, and been in business in Leeds, or somewhere, maybe even London. But I don't want to live away, I don't want to be down in the south. However, there's been years when your wages have been paid with what I could save out of works in Leeds, and there's been years now since there's been any new machinery up in this quarry, because I daredn't spend it just then. It's been my fault you've been blaming Tommy for what's gone wrong, and it was Tommy gave me this black eye last night for it, because I've been ready to shift the blame to him, because if it was on me these last few weeks I'd not have been able to borrow any more money to pay the wages I could. Aye, you can blame me, but remember there was a year when all the stone we sent out didn't get paid for because a builder went bankrupt. If we'd gone bankrupt then after him there'd be no work here at all, and wouldn't have been this long time. I've done what I can, because I live here, I want the village to be my home. But by the time last night came I knew I was bankrupt too. I couldn't raise another penny of cash, and there wouldn't be any wages for this week; you'd have worked for nowt. Tommy gave me a black eye for a report I'd had printed that blamed him for sticking to brass over the years. But he never had the brass to stick to, and no one but Tommy ever saw the report; I just had it made so that I could raise cash on it but the chance didn't come. Here's a letter just come for me, that I haven't opened yet," and he pulled the registered envelope from his pocket. "It's to say I'm to be bankrupted and haven't to have any say in the quarry, haven't to interfere, haven't to manage. I'll be finished and out of business. I haven't been able to last through long enough to see everything right. Now, you know what there is between Marrick Lantho and me. We'd been friends once, and then fell out when the Irishwoman chose me, and then she went away from me when I was getting over-rich. Lantho knew as much about my affairs as I did, I reckon. But he wouldn't come in and help and have a share. He was a man who went his own way, and I could say nowt to him, nor him to me; he was constant in that, but variable in plenty of things. He didn't care for me, but he saw where I was fast against time. He knew what we needed to keep going, and I knew it too, but I couldn't do anything about it. I wanted rid of that house. I tried selling it but they didn't want it. But Lantho blew it down this morning, and got himself killed at it, thinking my lass was in it still. And it's done the trick, because there's the insurance money to come off it, and I'll not build a house with it, but pay off and settle about the quarry, and see whether the house gets built some other time. I'm off to town by the next train and give them their letter back and put it all right if I can. But listen, it's mebbe a waste to work today, and you'd all best go home and you'll get your money just the same. I mean, if

179

you don't get any you don't, but if there's some to come it'll count as a day's work, and you'll not want to when a man's been killed on the Incline."

Mason had been getting further and further away from Jedediah during the last words of the talk. He had begun to slip down the Incline with the Bank key, to be at work before Mr Stewart came. When he came to the bottom he could see, but not hear, Jedediah on the loaded wagon. There was no one working at the dock. Mason walked along the road into the village, scratching at the ked bites, wondering about his lost breakfast.

There was nothing to be done about breakfast, in the way of getting a proper meal. He thought of buying biscuits or chocolate, and then thought they would be too difficult to eat. He came to the Bank, half supposing that Lantho would be there, leaning back on his stool and finding out where he had been. No Lantho was there. The door was locked. Mason unlocked it himself, and went in. He picked up the letters and put them on Lantho's desk, then thought that was no use and put them on his own. But that was not right. He took them through into Mr Stewart's room and put them there. He could not open them himself.

He locked the outer door again, before going out to the back of the Bank and washing his face. Green light looked back at him from the mirror, and yesterday's scratched cheek. He pulled his fingers through his hair, dried on the towel smelling faintly of Lantho, and went back to his own desk, after unlocking the door but not pulling the blind so that it snapped up.

He got out the books he was working on and began work. He was adding up and thinking of other things. He came to the bottom of a page and wrote in a total without knowing what he had done, that it had been done. All the figures meant nothing, and ticked themselves off without speaking, like white beans falling in a row, some arithmetic game he had played with at school; he did not know what it had been then.

The whole book he was working at was unreal, and began to hold no more meaning than the wood it was made from. It was wood sawn fine into a different kind of leaf from the kind nature would grow. On these thin leaves were marks. The marks were marks made by insects and ought not to be there; a perfect tree would be without the disease. But Mason's pen went on infecting each page as he came to it, while his mind hovered now at the Incline, now by the sawing sheds watching the fight, now at the mystery of the rocks and their transformation by the mist and one bird singing and their restoration to the commonplace and laughable by the flying of another bird. In his thoughts he wondered where Moira had gone, why she was not part of them. He tried to think consciously of her, but when he did he made a silly mistake in his figures, writing down the number he had not added up, putting something else entirely, as if his writing arm, but not his brain, had become insane. He had to scrub out the mistake and write the same mistake in again. Now he was truly mad, thoroughly mad. And still he had not thought of Moira except as a name, so that he was failing in every way.

Mr Stewart came in. Mason stood up, and was said good morning to. Mr Stewart went through to his own office. In a little while he called for Mason. He went through.

"Lantho not back yet?" he asked. "He went early yesterday, and comes late today. And now we need him more than ever.

And what's all the excitement in the village, folk milling about and talking? And what's the matter with you, Mason? You look as if you'd slept in your clothes, and seen a ghost. And why does the office smell like a flock of sheep?"

Mason was saved from answering by a knocking at the outside door. He went to see what it was, because anyone who really wanted attention out of opening hours could have come in and been said sarcastic things to by Lantho. It was the policeman, to see Mr Stewart. He had missed him at the train, and came now to have a word with him. He carried the bag of papers Lantho had taken yesterday, that he had left in the quarry house today. Mason took him straight through to Mr Stewart, and sat down to his papers again, having to think of each figure as he saw it, unable to consider anything else at the same time.

Five minutes later Mr Stewart came out. "You should have told me," he said. "I don't know whether either of us will do any banking, Mason. Lantho's played his last joke, I think, and been hoist by his own petard, just exactly. I'm shutting up shop now, so you go home, and when we open again, if we do, I'll send for you. There's bound to be some work, even if we close, because we'll have to show our books. But we'll not be open to the public for a bit. Go on, off you go, lad." He took a pound note from his pocket and put it in Mason's pocket. "That'll get you home," he said.

XV

ON A MONDAY morning ten days later there was a whistling like the calls of prehistoric birds on the road east of the quarry. The whistling echoed from the far side of the dale and among the empty tips of the quarry. Mason walked on with Dad to meet the whistling.

It came from three black traction engines, road locomotives, full of fire and steam, hauling long trailers, hung with shovels and buckets and chains, immense on the hillside under the banking walls of the tips, stalking through the uninhabited wasteland to its cold centre, the idle sawing-shed, and the black smithy beyond. No men had worked for more than a week. The boilers were dry, the fires drawn, the driving belts stiff, the shafts still in their bearings. The engines came proudly in as if they were pulling a roundabout, as if at any moment there might be steam music, tunes to wake stone, marches to bring the gangs to work again.

The engines had been expected. They did indeed bring the gangs, but only smiths and engineers, led by Bucko Robinson. The engines drew up the trailers outside the smithy. Following them were the eight horses of the quarry, making it more like a circus. The unloading began. The trailers held all the parts for a new ten ton crane, of ten foot gauge, like the broken one but thirty years younger. It was brought out piece by piece, hauled to a railhead made for it, and assembled. Before it had been completed the engines went away, their work done, whistled at the road, and climbed the hill, and could be heard whistling down the dale for the rest of the day.

The new crane was one of the more obvious signs of new things in the village. Mason had been off work for a week, and now went down in the afternoons. Mr Stewart had done all the other work himself, and explained to Mason how a new company had been formed from the remains of Jedediah's holdings, with the money from the insurance company. Mason did not know what the words meant that Mr Stewart used, but kept them by in case he found their meanings in use at any time.

A new director came and talked to Dad. He was very young, Dad thought, and came from somewhere south of Leeds. Dad found he knew what he was talking about. Stuff you could see, he thought, was better than words and figures, like the ones Mason had tried to make him understand about the new company. If there was going to be stone brought out that would assure Dad better than about capital and management.

Notices went up in the village, that the gangs would be wanted on the next Monday, that pay would be given daily for the first week, if needed, that for the first week the company would provide a cheap meal at noon. On Thursday, before that day, Mr Stewart told Mason that he would be in charge of paying the men the daily money for that first fortnight, and after that the wages would be paid through the Bank, and Mason would be in charge until a more senior clerk was appointed. It was not right, Mr Stewart said, to have a boy his age in charge of as much money as a week's wages for all the men, but it would have to be so until the new company, or whoever was in charge now, decided whether the Bank was going to pay, and whether the quarry was.

On Saturday the fires of the sawing shed and the smaller cranes were lit. Fresh clean coal came up, dragged by the horses, and made a fresh clean smoke. Mam, doing some late washing, was quite glad to see the smuts smearing the linen on the line. The shot-firer came along and drilled his holes. No one had heard blasting since Bishopside Hall fell.

"Seven o'clock Monday," said the shot-firer.

"Seven o'clock Monday," said Dad.

"Seven o'clock Monday," said Mason, to the baker opposite the Bank. He was taking in the order for bread for the cheap meal Mam was to make ready for the quarry men who wanted it. He took payment in advance from the Bank, astonished at the amount it cost to buy simple stuff like bread.

"Seven o'clock Monday," said Lizzy Holmes, who was now taken on behind the counter at the bakery. Perhaps there were rats there more than anywhere else.

On Monday morning Mam came in and opened the windows. Through it came the noise of the quarry horses coming to work. There was a different horse noise too, of the baker's cart bringing the bread. It trembled when the shots went. Dad stepped across to the sawing shed and blew a long blast on the whistle. It was answered by the new crane.

Dad went into the office then and checked on the men as they came. Mason was there with him to sort the cards on this first day. In the middle of them came someone Mason had not seen since Lantho died. Jedediah Spitalhouse came up in the queue with the other men, and got himself signed on as a workman, dressed ready for it in boots and cap and leather shoulders to his jacket, and bootlaces round his trousers below his knees.

"Well now, Jedediah," said Dad, "I'm none so sure I'll take thee on. You might know overmuch about the business."

"I've not forgotten how to dig and shift muck," said Jedediah. "I've not smoked a cigar in weeks, and all the brass I get is what I can make with my own hands. There's nowt else. I'm not proud, or any daft thing like that."

"I'll put you in a gang," said Dad. "There'll be a long way to go before I can put you up at all, because you're new here."

"It's right," said Jedediah. "I'll work. I've forgotten how, but I'll frame, one way and another."

"There'll be no favours," said Dad. "But stop back tonight, Jed, and we'll go up the hill."

"Aye," said Jed. "Happen."

Dad meant the Nanny Goat Inn. Jedediah had hesitated a fraction before he answered. Mason thought he detected in that a memory of the coloured drinks in the cut bottles, with their names round their necks, crushed now and seeing no light, down the hill.

"That's more than I would do," said Dad. "I'd be proud. But he's right, what's there in pride? It's a sin, when all's said, the first of them. But Jed won't stop so long ganging. He'll be off after something."

He told Mam about it at breakfast. She had had hers and was using the whole of the middle room for a place to spread out helpings of cold food, cutting and cutting at bread and cheese.

"He'll not go so fast," said Mam. "He's got the Irishwoman to think of now, and keeping her needs more than one think. If he does anything it'll be a small thing, or she'll be off."

"Or he'll make it look small to her," said Dad.

Mason went down to his work. Mr Stewart came now instead of Lantho from the first train, and let him in. Mason had brought with him the number of men who would want money at the end of the day. He spent part of the morning putting the money up ready, the same amount in each packet, and naming the packets from the list. He felt guilty at Jedediah's name. He told Mr Stewart of what had happened that morning.

"He's lodging," said Mr Stewart. "Over the river. He hasn't a roof of his own now; they took everything away from him. There may be something for him next year, when it's all sorted out, but he won't take anything now; he gave it all over to the new company. I think he only cared about the quarry, all the time, but it didn't make the money to keep him right with all his other affairs and he had to let it run down, and that brought him down with it. He only ever managed to get hold of it because it paid so little and the owners had better uses for their money. I wish we'd got Lantho now. He knows about business, or he did, and he would have known more if he'd stuck to it. But if he hadn't been killed he'd be in jail for doing what he did. I think he'd rather be dead. I don't know why he did it, if he was bound to be found out. But perhaps he wasn't going to be found out, if he was in your house when it happened."

"I hope he saw Moira before he died," said Mason, glad to be able to share her with someone else safely. "Or he would have thought he had killed her."

"They say your last thought stays with you," said Mr Stewart. "But how do they know?"

Mason had not seen Moira since Mam led her off on that day on the Incline. When he had come back early from the Bank she had gone. He had not heard from her or of her since. Now that Jedediah was living in lodgings he supposed that she had left the village for good. Jedediah would do what some of the men did, lodged during the week and went back to their families for the week end. He had given up hope of seeing her again, and his memory of her lived in an emptiness inside him, and belonged to the same class as his recollections of Lantho. Lantho he would not see again, for firm reasons; with thoughts of Lantho, in the office mostly, looking up at quiet times to see whether a word might come his way, there was always the pang of certainty. With recollections of Moira there was not the certainty, but something much more dulling to the senses, a necessity of not caring too hard because of not knowing. He could care as much as he liked about Lantho, and nothing would alter that death. But in caring about Moira it was always possible that she might appear and not want to be cared about. In fact, he had been wondering about speaking to Lizzy Holmes about more than bread for seven o'clock, or the meat pie he bought sometimes for his dinner.

Today he went across to the bakery and bought a pie, to eat warm in the office. "Rat pie, mebbe," he said, as Lizzy put it into the bag.

"Aye, mind it; it bites," said Lizzy. "Mason Ross."

He crossed the street again, with the pie sitting warm on his fingers the other side of the paper. Coming up the pavement was a plain stranger, a girl. It was Moira, carrying a little packet, and not the only one in the street doing so today.

"Hello," he said, holding the treasonable pie, and speaking as he wondered if he dared.

"Mason," she said. "It's nice to see you," and she looked very pleased too. "You've still got those scratches," she said. "On your face."

Mason rubbed his face. His fingers smelt of pie. "Aye, well," he said. "It's nothing."

"You'll always have them," said Moira. "Always. Why didn't you come to see me? I was only at Mummy's. Now we live here. Mason, I am pleased to see you."

"I'm pleased to see you," said Mason. "I got this pie for your Dad," and he gave her the pie in its bag, glad to do something for Jedediah.

"He'll like it," said Moira.

"I still love you," said Mason. "You know."

"I love you," said Moira. "You're all I've got left. I hope I see you again, now we live in the same town."

"We did before," said Mason.

"But it's different now," said Moira. "It is," and she began to walk on because she had to. "It's different like when that crow flew across and it wasn't a place where we shouldn't be, but earth again. Mason, I hope I see you every day."

He watched her go up the street and turn towards the lane. Then he went back to the bakery and asked Lizzy Holmes for a crow pie; "The last one got away."

"I rather thought it," said Lizzy. "I near as owt took a stick and stopped it for you."

Mason went out of the bakery feeling rich and sinful, not because of buying two pies, but because, somehow, he had two points of attachment for his heart, and Moira was the stronger one, but not the only one. Only she had marked him first.

*　　　*　　　*

189

Peter Ward was one who took his money on the first day. Mason thought it was not right, and said so. Peter had got himself a man's day's wage, more than he needed.

"We'll be off and get shot of it then," said Peter. "We've waited long enough, Mason. We'll get to the Nanny Goat Inn and do what we said."

"My Dad's off up there," said Mason. "I don't dare." But almost at once he was proved wrong, and he did dare. Peter had been the last to get his money, being a W, and when he went there was nothing more to do. Dad called across to Mason to go up with them and have his first drink. Jedediah said they would need bringing home, and better him than Mary. So they went up the hill, following the men.

"I've had bits of ale," said Peter. "But I've never got my own bought yet," and he rattled the coins in his pocket.

"I've been to the Nanny Goat Inn," said Mason. "With a girl. We had sixpennorth. I was sick."

Peter was properly silent at this double feat. "You'd have a bad head too, after," he said, when he had been properly silent long enough.

"Nowt to speak of," said Mason. He would have finished the joke properly and revealed truthfully that it had been milk, not ale, that he had drunk, but Jedediah started up a hare at his feet and they chased it vainly across the grass, and he forgot.

He found, when he came to the ale, at the Inn, that he would rather have milk than the flat sumpy stuff looking like the drainings from the sawing shed boiler. Peter, however, was sure he was going to like it, and drank two mugs while Mason sipped one. It was a fine evening and they sat outside, with the other quarrymen coming and going hastily, to be home with their day's pay before they were late enough to be blamed.

Peter finished his third mug, and went in to buy more for himself, Jedediah and Dad. Mason sipped the first still. Already he felt an obscuring dizziness that no one else seemed to feel. Dad and Jedediah, drinking twice as much, were only talking more loudly and seeing jokes that were not there. Peter came back with three mugs, drank his fast, and sat back on his bench, saying that he right enjoyed it. A quarryman gave the dog a mug of ale, which it had been asking for ever since they came.

Mason finished his ale, and sat there beside Peter feeling very dizzy but not unhappy. Peter was talking, and talking rubbish too, he heard. Then Peter went away suddenly, and came back in a while, saying he'd done it, over by the wall, and he'd better be going home now, he felt that bad. Mason got up. He felt much the same as usual, but thought perhaps the first inch in all over him was invisible. Otherwise he was complete.

Dad said, "Aye, we'll be off and all, eh Jedededed I can't remember your name Jededed, I don't think you got one."

"I lost it," said Jedediah. "I dropped it and they didn't know whose it was."

"That's clever," said Dad. "Lemme shake your hand, Jededed." Dad put out his left arm, the one with no hand to it, and went round the quarrymen there offering to shake their hands. Mason got behind him in the end and pushed him towards the gate.

"They're foolish," said Peter. "I do feel bad, Mason. I'm not drunk, you know; I just feel bad."

Now that he was got going, and Jedediah was beside him, Dad kept on very well, following the path downhill. Peter went on ahead of them, saying he was off home, he didn't like drunk folk. He became darker in the rising darkness. Dad and Jedediah sang together, and the sun set ahead of them. Mason walked at the end of their shadows and felt the cool of the night coming on him, and heard the birds whipping the twilight with their cries. The dog at the Inn cried out too. Mason looked all round him. Somewhere in the grey rough edges of the hills lay the rocks he and Moira had visited, where he had had his second understanding of the world. Now he wanted a third, and all the still evening might have brought on, between the coloured heap of clouds on the sunset and the peaceful dark coming up the dale. But no vision was given to him then. Instead, when he came home he walked on the edge of the tips and looked down on the town, hearing Jedediah walking down the lane, and following him in his mind down to the bridge, over it, and to unknown houses in one of which was Moira. He thought glancingly of Lizzy, but knew it was another betrayal, a sort of cowardice. Lizzy could not hurt him, but Moira could, present or absent.

"Moira," he said, and watched the lights go out in the streets below until Mam called him in for his tea "or whatever meal you fancy it is."

"Goodnight," he shouted into the dusk. "Goodnight." An echo replied; or was it somebody's thought?